Clint Adams mounted the stairs . . .

He moved to his room and unlocked the door. His hand rested on the butt of the modified double-action Colt revolver on his right hip. The Gunsmith had enemies he didn't even know about. He always had to be alert and ready for danger. Survival often depended on vigilance . . .

Don't miss any of the lusty, hard-riding action in the
Charter Western series, THE GUNSMITH:

And coming next month:
THE GUNSMITH #41: HELL WITH A PISTOL

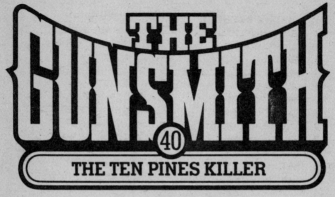

THE GUNSMITH

40

THE TEN PINES KILLER

J. R. ROBERTS

CHARTER BOOKS, NEW YORK

THE GUNSMITH #40: THE TEN PINES KILLER

A Charter Book/published by arrangement with
the author

PRINTING HISTORY
Charter Original/May 1985

ISBN: 0-441-30941-0

Charter Books are published by The Berkley Publishing Group,
200 Madison Avenue, New York, New York 10016.
PRINTED IN THE UNITED STATES OF AMERICA

To
Stuart and Sylvia Varon

ONE

The bitter cold wind seemed to knife through Clint Adams' sheepskin jacket. The chill seeped into his flesh to scrape icy talons across his bones. Clint Adams despised the cold almost as much as he hated to be called the Gunsmith.

The weather was an inescapable condition due to the time of year and regional location of Carsontown. Late November in Utah is seldom sunny and warm. As for being called the Gunsmith, that was another inescapable condition which had begun more than a decade earlier when a newspaper man labeled Clint with the monicker.

Clint had been a young deputy sheriff when he was first called the Gunsmith. The newspaper man had given him the title because Deputy Adams repaired and modified firearms as a hobby. However, the Gunsmith was more famous for his lightning fast draw and uncanny accuracy with a six-gun. The Gunsmith legend seemed to attract young gunhawks, looking to make a reputation for themselves, but whenever an eager youth forced Clint to defend himself, the challenger wound up in Boot Hill.

The Gunsmith decided he could no longer continue to do his job as he saw fit, so Clint turned in his badge and started a new profession. Ironically, the only other trade he knew was gunsmithing, so he bought a wagon

and converted it into a combination traveling home and
gunsmith shop.

Clint drifted throughout the West, making his living
as a gunsmith. Occasionally circumstances lured him
into a brief job which required his prowess with a
pistol, but the Gunsmith tried to lead a peaceful, quiet
life—most of the time. Clint's natural curiosity and
thirst for adventure actually got him in as much trouble
as his unwanted reputation as a "gunfighter."

The Gunsmith had traveled to Utah in search of more
business for his gunsmith trade. Clint had been pleased
to find quite a few customers in Carsontown. The
people had been friendly enough and almost a dozen
men needed some work done on their guns.

However, Clint had spent more time in Utah than he
had intended. The profits he'd made so far wouldn't do
him much good if he froze to death on the trail. The
Gunsmith had once endured a blizzard in Montana,*
and he realized that the merciless winter cold could kill
a man as dead as any bullet.

He clenched a gloved fist to his jacket, pulling it
snugly around his body. He ducked his head low, using
the broad brim of his stetson and the turned-up collar
of his sheepskin garment to protect his face. Clint
squinted his eyes as he gazed at the wall of snow which
formed a dense fog throughout Carsontown. The
windswept snow reduced visibility. The surrounding
buildings became little more than large, obscure
shapes in the snow.

"Christ," Clint muttered through chattering teeth.
"And this is just a light snow flurry."

He managed to recognize the sign of the local sa-

_____

*The Gunsmith #12: The Canadian Payroll

loon. At that moment, Clint couldn't think of anything more appealing than a shot of whiskey to combat the awful cold. He hurried across the street. Frozen mud crackled under his boots.

The Gunsmith reached the plankwalk and found the batwings. He pulled them aside and slipped through the inner door which had been closed to keep out the icy, flying snow. Clint shut the door and glanced about the barroom.

The place was deserted except for the Gunsmith and Pete, the bartender. Clint liked the saloon. It had a long wooden bar with a leather-topped counter and several tables and chairs. A potbellied stove kept the room warm. An unusual feature in a frontier saloon, a platform surrounded by footlights, stood at the east wall. Clint had been in the saloon before, but he had never seen a performer on that stage.

Pete was busy tearing a poster off a wall. Clint had noticed the poster before. It advertised a performance by Thurgood Gerard, noted Shakespearean actor, who was supposed to make a trip to Utah to perform in *The Tragedy of Hamlet, Prince of Denmark*. The poster bore a drawing of Gerard, a gaunt man with hollow cheeks and a hawk-billed nose. The actor wore a black wig and dark clothing, and he held a human skull in his right hand.

"I take it Mr. Gerard won't be playing here after all," the Gunsmith remarked.

"Oh," Pete said, turning to face the Gunsmith. "Howdy, Clint. Didn't hear you come in. Care for a drink?"

"Anything that'll thaw out my belly," Clint replied.

"How about some brandy?" Pete asked.

"Brandy?" the Gunsmith raised an eyebrow. "I

haven't drank brandy for over a year. Hardly remember what it tastes like.''

"Come on over to the bar, and I'll give you somethin' to refresh your memory,'' Pete offered.

"Best suggestion I've heard all day,'' the Gunsmith replied as he followed Pete to the bar. "By the way, was that poster genuine or was it meant as a joke?''

"You're from back East, ain't you?'' the bartender inquired as if asking Clint if he had a dreadful, contagious disease.

"Guilty,'' the Gunsmith replied. "But I've been living out West for more than half my life.''

"Yeah,'' Pete began as he moved behind the bar. "But you was still educated back East. Probably figure anybody who was born and raised in these parts has to be pig ignorant.''

"Hell, Pete,'' Clint sighed, "I know better than that. Still, I wouldn't figure too many folks in Carsontown would be interested in a Shakespearean play. Especially one performed by an Eastern city slicker and probably a Yankee snob to boot.''

"Thurgood Gerard is from Virginia,'' Pete stated, placing two balloon glasses and a bottle of brandy on the counter. "I understand he was a captain in the Confederate Army, so he ain't no Yankee. He's an actor, so maybe he's a snob.''

"Do you know Shakespeare?'' Clint asked.

"The Merchant of Venice,'' Pete replied proudly. He cleared his throat and said, "Act One. Antonio says: 'In sooth I know not why I am sad, It wearies me, and you say it wearies you. But how I got it, found it or . . . er . . . come to get it. What stuff 'tis made of, whereof it is born.' ''

"Not bad,'' the Gunsmith nodded.

"Might'a got a word or two wrong," Pete shrugged. "But I've read *The Merchant of Venice* about a hundred times. Got most of it memorized. I know *Hamlet* and *Macbeth* pretty good too. Lots of folks are fond of Bill Shakespeare here in Carsontown."

"Well, don't get the wrong idea," Clint began. "I don't figure folks in Utah are stupid or uneducated, and I think it's real fine that you folks have an interest in literature and all . . ."

"But why would there be so many Shakespeare readers in Carsontown?" Pete guessed. "Well, you see we got a school teacher who offered a readin' course to adults. A lot of us went to it. Makes sense that we should be able to read as well as our own kids can, right?"

"And this school teacher got you fellas interested in Shakespeare," the Gunsmith mused. "A little culture never hurt anybody."

"We really learned to like Shakespeare," Pete frowned. "And we were sure lookin' forward to gettin' to see *Hamlet* performed by Thurgood Gerard and Company."

"Gerard isn't exactly Edwin Booth," Clint remarked. "I never heard of him before."

"He's a professional stage actor," Pete answered. "That's what matters. We've all read Shakespeare, but we never got to see it performed. We sure won't get to now."

"Maybe Gerard will come out here in the spring when the weather improves," Clint suggested.

"Weather ain't the problem," Pete sighs. "Got a telegraph message this morning. A representative from the acting company informed me that Thurgood Gerard is unavailable. According to the telegraph, Gerard has just disappeared. Probably an excuse for not makin' the trip.''

"In the meantime, why don't you folks perform some Shakespeare with local talent?'' Clint asked.

"You mean *us* do *Hamlet* instead?''

"Or whatever play you and your friends decide on,'' Clint nodded. "Why not?''

"That might just work out, Clint,'' Pete said happily. "I'll have to talk it over with the others, but I think they'll be turnin' handsprings over the idea.''

"Just sorry I'll miss the performance,'' the Gunsmith stated.

"You plan to leave soon?'' the bartender asked with a frown. "Well, I reckon you've about wrapped up your business here. Can't say as I blame you for wanting to get out of Utah before the first big snowfall.''

"Yeah,'' Clint replied. "If this flurry doesn't let up, I think I'll head south and forget about Ten Pines.''

"Ten Pines?'' Pete raised his eyebrows. "That's a mighty small town. Folks there keep to themselves most of the time. I met a young feller from Ten Pines once. He didn't talk much. Seemed to get sort of uncomfortable when I asked him what his town was like. Feller said it was time to leave. Said he *needed* to get out of Ten Pines. Reckon the place hasn't grown much over the last ten years.''

"Maybe,'' Clint said as he sipped his brandy. "But I still might find some guns that need repair. They don't have a gunsmith in Ten Pines, do they?''

"Not that I know of,'' the bartender answered.

"Then it might be worth a trip,'' Clint declared. "At least, I sure hope so.''

TWO

Adams left the saloon. A thin blanket of snow covered the ground. Every rooftop was laced with white streaks. Flakes of snow continued to drift down from the sky, but the flurry and the vicious wind had subsided.

Clint jogged across the street to the livery stable, and entered the building. Jeb, the local hostler, was seated near a stove. Dressed in overalls and a long-john shirt, the middle-aged liveryman was leafing through a copy of the *Police Gazette*. Obviously, not everyone in Carsontown was fond of Shakespeare. Jeb didn't appear to be much of a reader either. He just liked to look at the pictures.

"Oh, howdy, Clint," the hostler said, rising from his stool. "What can I do for you?"

"Just want to check on my wagon and animals," the Gunsmith explained. "I'll be leaving in the morning."

"Sure thing, Clint," Jeb nodded. "I've been takin' extra-special care of your rig and them critters. Followed your instructions just like you told me."

"Glad to hear it, Jeb," Clint said as he strolled over to his wagon.

The vehicle was in good condition. Jeb had greased the axles of the wheels and even replaced a frayed rein. Nothing inside the rig had been disturbed. Clint checked the two team horses. The animals had been well-fed and watered. Finally, the Gunsmith moved to the stall where Duke was kept.

Duke was a magnificent, glossy black Arabian gelding. To Clint, Duke was more than an animal. The big, powerful horse was intelligent, loyal, and courageous. Duke seemed to possess all the best abilities of a human being, but none of the flaws. Small wonder the Gunsmith regarded Duke as a friend and companion rather than just a beast of burden.

"How you doing, big fella?" Clint inquired as he entered the stall.

Duke neighed in an excited manner and lowered his head. Clint scratched the animal's neck and ears. Duke rubbed his snout against Clint's chest.

"You seem pretty good, fella," Clint remarked, combing the animal's mane with his fingers. "But I bet you're ready to get out of here and get a little exercise, aren't you, Duke?"

The gelding neighed in reply. Duke raised and lowered his head as if to answer Clint's question. The Gunsmith found a brush and spent half an hour grooming his prize horse. After spending some time with Duke, Clint returned to the hotel.

Jessie Hinton, the desk clerk, smiled at the Gunsmith. An attractive redhead, Jessie had responded quite favorably to Clint's flirting and flattery. The Gunsmith had hoped to convince her to join him in his room, but apparently there wouldn't be enough time to woo the lady. Pity, Clint thought. But there would be other towns and other women.

"How do you like the weather, Clint?" Jessie asked cheerfully.

"Wonderful," he replied dryly, shaking snow off

the brim of his stetson, "if you like cold and damp."

"Winter ain't even started yet," the woman told him.

"I know," the Gunsmith nodded. "That's why I'm going to make a fast trip up to Ten Pines and then head south to do the rest of my business in a warmer climate."

"Oh," Jessie frowned. "When will you leave, Clint?"

"Tomorrow," he replied. "Early. About dawn."

"Well," she sighed. "Sure been nice havin' you for a guest at the hotel."

"And it's sure been nice getting to know a pretty lady like you," Clint said with a grin. "Sorry we couldn't get to know each other better."

"Me too," the woman agreed sadly.

Clint Adams mounted the stairs to the next story. He moved to his room and unlocked the door. His hand rested on the butt of the modified double-action Colt revolver on his right hip. The Gunsmith had enemies he didn't even know about. He always had to be alert and ready for danger. Survival often depended on vigilance.

The Gunsmith opened the door cautiously and entered. He quickly checked the room, his hand still resting on the grips of his forty-five. However, Clint found nothing of danger lurking within his quarters. Clint relaxed and moved to a chest of drawers.

He removed some spare clothing from the drawers and began to stuff them into a saddlebag. Clint reached behind the cabinet and retrieved a small pistol wrapped in an oil cloth. He unwrapped the weapon and inspected it. A .22-caliber New Line Colt was an ideal "hold-out" weapon. Clint often wore it tucked in his belt, hidden under his shirt. However, he had not felt a need for the "belly gun" while he was in Carsontown.

There was a knock on the door. Clint turned, his hand once again dropping to the .45 Colt on his hip. He approached the door slowly and stood clear in case someone on the opposite side decided to pump a couple bullets through it.

"Clint?" a familiar female voice called softly. "It's me, Jessie."

"Just a second," Clint replied, hastily stuffing the little New Line pistol into his saddlebag.

The Gunsmith opened the door. The pretty redhead entered. She smiled up at Clint. He slowly closed the door. To Clint's delight, the woman did not ask him to leave it open.

"This is a nice surprise," the Gunsmith remarked. "What can I do for you, Jessie?"

"I just wanted to say good-bye properly," she explained.

The woman leaned closer and began to press her lips to his cheek. Clint turned his head and kissed her firmly on the mouth. It was a bold move, but Jessie did not object. Clint's arms snaked around Jessie and pulled her closer as they lingered in the passion of the kiss.

The Gunsmith's hands gradually moved to Jessie's round breasts. He stroked them gently, feeling the nipples harden beneath the fabric of her dress. The woman gently broke the embrace, and walked to the side of the bed and began to remove her clothing.

Clint admired the alabaster smoothness of her bare flesh. Jessie's neck was long and graceful. Her breasts were compact, but perfectly formed and capped by pink nipples. Her waist was lean, and her legs were long and beautifully shaped.

The Gunsmith stripped off his clothes as well. Jessie sat on the mattress and watched. She liked what she saw. Clint Adams' tall, lean frame was well-muscled. Numerous scars marred his flesh, mostly tattoos from bullets which had creased his skin. The most obvious of these was the jagged scar on the Gunsmith's left cheek.

He joined Jessie on the bed. Skilled fingers caressed her skin. She cooed with pleasure as Clint lowered his lips to her breasts. He kissed them gently and licked the stiff nipples. His mouth closed around a nipple as he sucked, teasing it with his teeth and tongue. His hands continued to slide along her body until they found her thighs.

The woman moaned happily as Clint's fingers stroked her thighs. His deft fingers shifted to her triangle of love, gently probing the lips of her vagina. She gasped when he inserted a finger.

"I'm ready, Clint," Jessie rasped.

Clint didn't rush. He moved his hand back and forth. Her womb was wet and warm. The woman groaned, shifting her hips to receive his thrusting finger. The Gunsmith decided she was indeed ready.

He mounted Jessie. Her fingers found his manhood and gripped the erect pole of flesh. She stroked it lovingly and guided his member to the center of her womanhood.

The Gunsmith rotated his hips to slowly work his penis deeper. Jessie thrust her loins up, drawing him in. Clint responded by increasing the speed of his pounding cock. She trembled and quivered beneath him, rapidly approaching her climax.

Clint realized she was about to come and rammed himself home. She cried out as a wild orgasm bolted through her body. The Gunsmith continued to kiss her and stroke her breast before he began to pump his member inside her once more.

The woman cried out again and wrapped her arms around his neck. Jessie's legs hugged his hips as the second orgasm overwhelmed her. She bucked like a bronco while the Gunsmith disgorged the hot load from his throbbing penis.

"Oh, Clint," Jessie whispered after a few minutes. "You sure know how to say good-bye."

THREE

"I have to get back to the front desk," Jessie explained as she reluctantly climbed out of bed. "Don't want to lose my job."

"You mean I'm going to have to sleep in this cold, empty bed all by myself tonight?" the Gunsmith inquired as he watched her pull on her clothing.

"Not if I can help it," Jessie smiled. "But I won't be able to get back up here until after nine o'clock. Don't get yourself too tuckered out until I get back."

The woman left. Clint fished a turnip watch from his pants-pocket. It was only six-ten. With almost three hours to kill before Jessie would return, the Gunsmith decided to get dressed and pay a quick visit to the saloon.

Clint Adams braved the cold and ventured from the hotel. The snow had stopped, but the frigid wind had returned. The Gunsmith turned up the collar of his sheepskin jacket and quickly shuffled across the street to the saloon.

The tavern was now full of customers. Clint couldn't find a vacant table in the place, let alone one which would allow him to put his back to the wall. The Gunsmith never exposed his back when he sat down in a saloon, a rule he had learned from James "Wild Bill"

13

Hickok. Unfortunately, Hickok had broken his own commandment and it cost him his life.*

Clint walked to the bar. He noticed a large, heavily muscled man standing on the stage. The man wore a dark shirt and trousers. His hands twitched nervously as he spoke in a loud, if trembling voice.

"And spur my dull revenge!" the man stated. "What is a man, if his chief good and market of his time be but to sleep and feed? A beast, no more."

"Hello, Clint," Pete, the bartender greeted. "Want some more brandy?"

"Just a beer," the Gunsmith replied. "Isn't that fella on the stage reciting *Hamlet*?"

"Sure is," Pete said cheerfully. "That's Jethro Kwanski, the town blacksmith. Knows his *Hamlet*, don't he? 'Course he ain't used to talkin' in front of folks."

"Looks like the audience enjoys it," Clint commented, although he noticed a pair of cowboys in the front row who were giggling over the blacksmith's performance.

"That capability and . . . er . . . god-like reason to fust in us unused," Jethro continued. "Now, whether it's bestial oblivion, or some craven scruple . . ."

"What the hell are you talkin' about, Jethro?" one of the cowboys demanded.

"He don't know," the other cowhand laughed.

"Uncouth jackasses," Pete hissed angrily. "Jethro and a couple others liked your idea so much that they couldn't wait to start practicing a few lines tonight."

---

*The Gunsmith #14: Dead Man's Hand

"Just don't blame me if things don't work out," the Gunsmith remarked.

"I'll pay for Mr. Adams' beer, feller," a voice announced.

The Gunsmith turned to face the speaker. A tall, whip-thin man with a ferret face and a trim, black mustache leaned against the bar. His eyes resembled cold, black stones.

"Obliged, friend," Clint said as Pete placed a beer mug on the counter.

"My pleasure, Mr. Adams," the man with the icy black eyes said with a smile. "I don't reckon you remember me, but our paths crossed once before."

"Oh, I remember you," the Gunsmith replied. "You're Frank Cameron."

"I'm flattered you know who I am, Mr. Adams," Cameron stated. "Bartender, I'll have a beer, too."

"Comin' up, feller," Pete said.

"We were in Dalton City a couple years ago," Clint told Cameron. "We were never introduced, but I saw you call Wade Kingsley into the street. You beat him to the draw and killed him with one bullet. Through the heart, right?"

"You got a good memory," Cameron said. "Kingsley was fast. He'd taken a lot of men before he faced me that day."

"But you were faster," the Gunsmith remarked. "Do me a favor and call me Clint."

"Sure enough," Cameron nodded. "And you can call me Frank. Like to keep things friendly between us."

"I don't see why that should be a problem," the Gunsmith replied. "I understand you're a professional gunman. You never take on a fella just to add to your reputation.''

"That's right," Cameron confirmed. "I only kill folks for money. Nobody has hired me to take you on. To be honest, I'd just as soon nobody ever does. I figure you and me are probably pretty close. Maybe I'm faster. Maybe you're faster. I can live without knowing the answer—and maybe I'd die if I found out. Besides, I've followed your career and I admire you, Clint. Wouldn't want to kill you.''

"Glad to hear it, Frank," the Gunsmith replied.

"I just get a little concerned when I see a feller with your reputation in a town the size of Carsontown," the gunfighter replied. "Wonder if maybe somebody hired you.''

"I'm just here to make a profit as a traveling gunsmith," Clint assured him. "Despite what you might have heard, that's how I make my living. If it makes you feel any better, I'm moving on tomorrow anyway.''

"Then let me buy you another drink," Cameron urged.

"This round is on me," the Gunsmith stated. "Pete? How about a couple more beers?''

"You got it, Clint," the bartender answered.

Jethro Kwanski continued to recite *Hamlet*. The blacksmith's face was red with embarrassment and anger as the two cowhands in the front row kept heckling his performance.

"Whereon the numbers cannot try the cause," Jethro declared. "There ain't tomb enough or country to hide the slain . . .''

"You'd better keep makin' horseshoes and forget

about this play-actin' stuff, you dumb son of a bitch,''
one of the cowboys howled with laughter.

"O, from this time forth," Jethro began as he
stepped off the stage and approached the two cowhands. "My thoughts be bloody, or be nothing
worth!''

"Oh, shit,'' one of the cowboys bolted from his
chair.

Jethro charged forward and seized the heckler's shirt
before the cowhand could escape. The blacksmith's
other hand grabbed the cowboy's belt. He picked up
his tormentor as if the cowboy was just a bag of grain.

"Sweet Jesus,'' the other cowhand rasped. He held
a bottle of whiskey by its neck and prepared to strike
Jethro with it.

The blacksmith suddenly hurled the first cowhand
across the table. The man screamed as his body sailed
into the second cowboy. Both hecklers crashed to the
floor. The whiskey bottle rolled harmlessly out of
reach.

"Now that's what I call a helluva show!'' a voice in
the audience cried out.

The barroom was abruptly filled by vigorous
applause. Jethro mounted the stage platform once
more. He turned to face his public and bowed.

FOUR

The Gunsmith returned to the hotel and waited in his room for Jessie to get off work. A few minutes after nine, the woman entered his room. They made love for hours, then drifted into a pleasantly exhausted sleep.

At dawn, Clint Adams rose and pulled on his clothes. He finished packing his saddlebags and left the hotel. Clint was glad the snow had ceased to fall, and the wind no longer slashed at him like an icy saber. The weather would probably change for the worse, but hopefully he'd be out of Utah before the first big blizzard. The Gunsmith headed for the livery, eager to get on the trail again.

Clint drove his wagon across the town limits of Carsontown. Duke followed the rig, attached to a guideline at the rear of the wagon. The Gunsmith consulted his map of the region as he headed north to his next destination.

The Gunsmith arrived at Ten Pines about noon. It wasn't much of a town. There were less than a dozen buildings in the community and Clint guessed the population to be less than twenty people—give or take a kid or two. Duke snorted, blowing twin streams of vapor from his nostrils.

"I know, big fella," Clint told the big black gelding. "There probably isn't enough business in a town this size to pay for the livery for you and this rig. But we're here now, so let's try to make the most of it.''

Duke responded by snorting again.

Clint drove the wagon into Ten Pines. Whether or not his prediction about the town was right, the Gunsmith still had to take care of his animals. He drove to the livery. A young man, dressed in a wool coat and a scarf wrapped around his head to cover his ears, emerged from the building.

"Hello, sir," the hostler greeted. "Do your animals need medical attention or merely shelter?"

"I reckon they're all healthy enough," Clint replied as he climbed down from the wagon. "Are you a veterinarian, fella?"

"That I am," the youth declared proudly. "My father, Dr. Harrimon Kirby, takes care of the sick people in Ten Pines. I take care of the animals. Medical care is sort of a tradition in my family. We reckon it's the most honorable profession, saving the lives of man and beast.''

"It's mighty important to feel what you do for a living is important," the Gunsmith stated.

"And what do you do for a living, Mr. . . .''

"Adams, Clint Adams. I'm sort of a gun doctor. Repair sickly firearms and modify others to function better.''

"Some of us help to save lives," Kirby said dryly. "Others help to take them. The only purpose of a gun is to kill.''

"What do you do with a horse with a broken leg, Doc?" Clint inquired. "Strangle it to death?''

"That isn't the same as carrying a gun on your hip in order to kill other men," Kirby insisted.

"Sometimes the only way to stay alive is to kill,''

the Gunsmith replied. "Folks were killing each other before guns were invented."

"I didn't mean to offend you, Mr. Adams," Kirby assured him. "What can I do for you, sir?"

"You can take care of my animals and my wagon for as long as I'm in town," Clint answered. "I'll pay extra to make sure it's worth your time and effort. Make sure you take good care of everything, especially Duke. He's the big black Arabian at the rear of my rig."

"A beautiful animal," Kirby said with sincere admiration.

"We can agree on that, Doc," Clint nodded.

"Let's see," the hostler scratched the side of his nose thoughtfully. "I'd say a dollar-fifty would be a reasonable price to look after your animals and that wagon. That's a dollar-fifty a day, of course."

"Reasonable, huh?" the Gunsmith muttered. "Well, I'll agree to the price, but you'd better take real good care of everything."

"Don't worry about that, Mr. Adams," Kirby urged as Clint paid him in advance. "Thank you."

The Gunsmith made certain his horses and the wagon were safely sheltered before he headed for the sheriff's office. A weary, middle-aged lawman with a balding pate glanced up from his desk. The sheriff's eyes were dark blue and surrounded by bags. He didn't seem very happy when he noticed the well-oiled Colt revolver hung low on Clint's hip.

"Somethin' I can do for you, stranger?" he inquired. The tone of his voice suggested he hoped the answer would be "No."

"Well," Clint began. "I used to be a deputy sheriff myself. I know a lawman likes to know when a stranger comes to town. Just figured I'd save you some trouble."

"Mighty considerate," the sheriff grunted. "What the hell are you, feller? Look like a gunfighter to me. What are you doin' in a little ol' town like Ten Pines? Not much call for gunfighters here. Not much tolerance for 'em neither."

"My name is Clint Adams, and I'm a traveling gunsmith."

"I've heard of you," the lawman snorted. "You're not a gunsmith. You're *the* Gunsmith."

"That's what some folks call me," Clint confessed.

"Way I hear it," the sheriff continued, "you're still a goddamn gunfighter."

"You heard wrong, friend," the Gunsmith replied.

"My name is Matt Connors," the sheriff told him. "And I ain't your friend. I hear you leave a bunch of dead bodies every place you go, Adams."

"I just left Carsontown this morning," Clint said with a shrug. "As far as I know, nobody died while I was there."

"Guess I ain't got call to run you outta town, Adams," Connors admitted. "At least not yet."

"Got a law against gunsmithing?" Clint asked.

"Got one against killin' people," Connors answered.

The Gunsmith heard the pounding of horse hooves on hard ground, accompanied by the rattle of wagon wheels. He glanced out the window and saw a stagecoach pull up in front of the hotel across the street.

The driver climbed down and opened the coach door while his partner laid down a Greener shotgun and began hauling down baggage from the luggage rack on the roof. Four figures emerged from the vehicle.

Clint couldn't see the newcomers very well. Three of the arrivals were men. Two of them were big, with massive chests and broad shoulders. The third was short and portly, his rotund frame cloaked in a heavy coat with a fur collar. All three wore derby hats which suggested they were Easterners.

However, the fourth passenger interested the Gunsmith. She was a young blonde woman. Her body was bundled up in a fur coat and both hands were covered by a muffler. Clint glimpsed a fair profile which hinted of classic beauty.

"Adams?" Sheriff Connors snapped. "You payin' attention to me or not?"

"Just noticed the stage arrived," Clint replied. "Looks like you've got four more strangers in town."

"Probably Harlan Marshall's sister and some of her family," Connors shrugged. "Harlan left her the general store in his will. She's supposed to arrive any day now."

"If she has," Clint mused, "Harlan had a fine looking sister."

"Kinda doubt that, Adams," the lawman commented. "Harlan Marshall was sixty-nine years old when he died. Imagine his sister must be close to that age, too."

"You got something against older women?" the Gunsmith inquired with a grin.

"Ain't got a lot of use for women period," Connors replied gruffly. "My goddamn wife run off with a whiskey drummer almost ten years ago. Never made the mistake of trustin' another female since."

"Hell of a decision," Clint remarked. "Cutting yourself off from half the human race that way. But, you live your life any way you please, Sheriff."

"You just watch how you live yours while you're in Ten Pines, Adams," Connors warned.

"Sure has been a pleasure talking to you, Sheriff," the Gunsmith said dryly. "Maybe we can have another nice little chat before I leave Ten Pines."

Clint left the sheriff's office and crossed the street. The stagecoach rolled out of town. Its driver cracked his whip above the heads of the team to urge the horses into a full gallop. Apparently he was eager to get out of Ten Pines, probably because he wanted to reach a stagecoach station before the weather got worse.

The Gunsmith walked along the plankwalk to the hotel. He opened the door and stepped into the hotel lobby. An owl-faced desk clerk stared at Clint, his features bleached with fear.

The portly newcomer leaned against the desk. His pudgy fingers were interlaced and rested on his chest. A smug smile was spread across his broad face and a confident twinkle gleamed in his sky-blue eyes.

The woman stood by the staircase. She was indeed lovely, with delicate features, large blue eyes and a milky fair complexion. Her figure was still concealed by the fur coat, but Clint suspected her body would not be a disappointment.

However, at the moment, Clint was more concerned about the two muscular, hard-faced men who stood at both sides of the doorway. Both men had a Police Colt in their fists, pointed at his heart.

"Come on in, Mister," the fat man invited, "and let's talk."

"How can I refuse an offer like that?" Clint replied as he raised his hands and stepped forward.

FIVE

"Get his gun, Crusher," the portly stranger ordered.

"Crusher?" the Gunsmith blinked with surprise.

"Get cute and you'll find out how I got the name," the big man said as he leaned forward and plucked the .45 Colt from Clint's holster.

Crusher was built like an oak tree stump. About five foot ten, he was four inches shorter than the Gunsmith, but he probably outweighed Clint by forty pounds. He didn't seem to have much fat on him either. Crusher's head was shaved, but his eyebrows were black and bushy. Clint almost expected the brute to bend the barrel off his modified Colt. The Gunsmith wouldn't have been surprised if Crusher was capable of such a feat.

"Listen up, fella," the portly man began as he took a cigar from his breast pocket. "I want to know who you are and what you want. If you don't answer me, my associates will take you apart like a goddamn insect. Do I make myself clear?"

"My name is Clint Adams," the Gunsmith replied. "And right now I'd like you fellas to explain why you jumped me."

"We ain't answerin' questions, cowboy," the other

bruiser snarled. "We'll ask and you'll answer. Those are the rules."

The second brute was taller than Crusher, but not quite as bulky. Most of his weight appeared to be in his upper torso. The man's nose was crooked, as if it had been broken more than once. Most of his front teeth were gold.

"Why did you come in this hotel, Adams?" the fat man asked, lighting his stogie.

"I want to get a room for the night," Clint answered. "What else?"

"You're just gonna make things hard on yourself, Adams," the round-bellied ringleader warned. "Ain't that right, boys?"

Suddenly, Crusher seized Clint from behind. The other hulk immediately swung a fist into Clint's stomach. The Gunsmith gasped as the blow knocked the wind from his lungs.

"Hold up a minute, Thrasher," the fat man announced. "Don't hit him again until he has another chance to answer my question."

"Jesus," Clint groaned. "If he hits me again I'll be more likely to puke on the floor than answer any questions."

"You might lose more than your lunch, fella," the portly man warned. "In case you don't recognize the names, these two fellas are George "Crusher" Krios and Charles "Thrasher" Thompson. Crusher was a top professional wrestler back in Chicago. Crusher could out-wrestle just about anybody."

As if to demonstrate, Crusher quickly twisted Clint's right arm behind his back. The Gunsmith clenched his teeth in pain as his wrist was shoved up to his shoulder blades.

"Thrasher is a pugilist," the leader continued. "He was one of the best prizefighters in Illinois—one of the top contenders for the state championship. They disqualified him for 'unsportsmanlike' conduct in the ring."

"All I did was to hit a referee," Thrasher said as he leaned toward the Gunsmith. "Like this!"

Thrasher's left fist slashed a short hook to Clint's jaw. The Gunsmith's head snapped to the side from the punch. His jawbone throbbed and his skin stung where the hard knuckles had struck.

"My God, Richard," the woman said urgently. "Don't let Thrasher beat this poor man to a pulp."

"Shuddup," the fat man snapped. "Adams was watchin' us from the sheriff's office. Watchin' like a hawk. Then he headed over here, probably to find out which room I'd be stayin' at."

"You're not my type, fella," the Gunsmith stated, moving his jaw from side to side to be certain nothing had been broken by the boxer's punch. "Besides, I don't even know who you are."

"The name is Richard O'Shea," the portly man declared. "I figured you already knew about me. You're probably a bounty hunter hired by those dago bastards back in Chicago."

"Why don't you ask the sheriff who I am and why I'm here?" Clint suggested.

"Thrasher," O'Shea began, "you head on over to the lawman's office and ask him about Adams. Crusher, hand me Adams' gun so I can cover him in case he decides to start any trouble."

"Start it?" Clint groaned. "I'm already right in the middle of it."

Thrasher opened the door and slipped outside.

Crusher removed one hand from Clint's arm in order to draw the Colt revolver from his belt. He used his other hand to pin Clint's wrist to his back and maintain the hammerlock hold.

"This has gone far enough," the desk clerk declared, a tremble riding on every word. "I will not stand by and watch you kill a man in cold blood."

"Then don't watch," O'Shea snapped, holding out a hand to receive the gun.

Crusher extended his arm, fist clenched around the barrel of Clint's modified Colt. The wrestler prepared to hand the gun to O'Shea, butt first. The Gunsmith figured this was the best chance he was likely to get so he'd better make his move.

Clint suddenly bent his left arm and thrust the elbow back in a fast, high stroke. Crusher grunted when the elbow crashed into his jaw. The Gunsmith pivoted to the right and shoved into the wrestler's chest. He kept moving and slipped loose of Crusher's hold.

O'Shea tried to snatch the Colt from Crusher's hand. Clint was faster. His right hand grabbed the revolver while his left fist jabbed into Crusher's chin. Clint wrenched the weapon from his opponent's grasp. O'Shea prepared to seize the Gunsmith, but Clint punted a boot into the fat man's belly.

O'Shea stumbled backward and collided with the desk. Crusher raised his hands, fingers arched like talons, as he prepared to launch himself at the Gunsmith. The double-action Colt whirled in Clint's hand. Suddenly his fist held the gun, index finger on the trigger, the muzzle pointed at Crusher's chest. The wrestler abruptly came to a halt.

"Come on," Clint invited. "If you think you're

tough enough to take a forty-five slug through the heart.''

"Don't do anything hasty," Crusher urged, but he smiled as he placed a hand to his jaw. "Say, you nailed me pretty good, Adams. Not many men have managed to break outta my hammerlock before.''

"Put your hands on top of your bald head," the Gunsmith ordered stiffly, "or I'll blow your brains out.''

The wrestler followed instructions. O'Shea reached inside his coat pocket. Clint shifted the aim of his Colt toward the fat man.

"Bring the hand out empty, O'Shea," the Gunsmith ordered. "And don't try shooting through your pocket. Unless you're one hell of a marksman, and you're used to shooting from the hip. You'll miss anyway. I won't.''

O'Shea raised his hand slowly. Crusher slowly stepped closer and began to slide his fingers from his bald pate. The Gunsmith barely glanced at him.

"Crusher," he sighed, "take two steps back and keep your hands on your head—unless you want to rush me and commit suicide.''

The wrestler muttered something under his breath, but he followed Clint's order to the letter. O'Shea slowly raised his hands to the top of his derby.

"Don't touch that hat," the Gunsmith snapped. "March over to the wall. Both of you. Hands against the wall, feet apart. I imagine you boys know the way to do it. The Chicago police have probably put you through the paces more than once.''

"Well, I'll be damned," the blonde whispered, an amused smile on her tempting red lips.

O'Shea and Crusher faced the wall in the spread-eagle position. The Gunsmith frisked them quickly, but carefully. He relieved Crusher of his Police Colt revolver and found a derringer in O'Shea's coat pocket.

"Happy now, Adams?" the fat man asked sourly.

"Not just yet," the Gunsmith replied as he snatched the derby from O'Shea's head.

Clint glanced inside the hat. Another tiny .22-caliber, single-shot derringer was held to the liner by clamps. The Gunsmith backed up to the desk and placed the confiscated weapons on the counter.

"Keep an eye on this stuff, will you?" he asked the clerk.

"Uh . . . yessir," the owl-like man agreed nervously.

"You're smarter than I figured, Adams," O'Shea commented. "Figure you're smart enough to make a deal with me?"

"Just shut up and stay where you are," the Gunsmith told him. "Ma'am, why don't you go upstairs and keep out of the line of fire in case there's any shooting?"

"I'm afraid I'll miss the show," she answered with a coy grin.

"Suit yourself, lady," Clint replied. "What's your name?"

"Sandra Michaels," she said, cocking an eyebrow with interest. "And you're name is Clint Adams, right?"

"Just call me Clint," he told her. "It's a pleasure to meet you, Sandra. Can't say much for the company you keep, but it's always nice to meet a beautiful lady."

The door opened and Thrasher entered. The boxer's mouth fell open in astonishment when he found himself staring into the muzzle of Clint's pistol. The Gunsmith gestured with the Colt, silently instructing Thrasher to join his companions at the wall.

"Are all Chicago hoodlums as clumsy as you jaspers?" the Gunsmith inquired as he frisked Thrasher.

"Put that gun away, and I'll show you how clumsy I am," the boxer snorted.

"You're so tough," Clint said as he took another Police Colt from the man's pocket. He also found a pair of brass knuckle dusters in another pocket. "And so stupid."

He suddenly shoved his left palm into the back of Thrasher's skull. The boxer's face was rammed hard into the wall. Thrasher howled with pain when his nose crushed against the unyielding surface.

"Now, tell them what the sheriff said about me," Clint ordered, "or I'll show you how rough I can get."

"I'll kill you, Adams," Thrasher hissed, blood dripping from his nostrils.

"Not if I kill you first," the Gunsmith said as he cocked the hammer of his pistol, "which I'm gonna do if you don't start talking."

"Sheriff says Adams was in his office just to let the local law know he was in town," Thrasher explained. "Seems Adams is a former lawman hisself. Now he's a gunfighter known as the Gunsmith. Supposed to be some sort of living legend around these parts."

"I'm not a gunfighter," Clint insisted. "I told Connors why I'm here."

"Relax, Adams," Thrasher said. "The sheriff said you claimed you was here as a traveling gunsmith. Claim you're just gonna fix folks' guns and move on.

Didn't seem to believe you."

"Did you ask Connors if I'd expressed any interest in any travelers from Chicago?" Clint inquired. "Or did that simple little question skip your feeble mind?"

"I asked him," Thrasher snapped. "Sheriff said the only traveler you seemed to be interested in was a blonde floozy who got off the stage."

"Who you callin' a floozy?" Sandra pouted.

"I'm just repeating what the sheriff said," Thrasher replied.

"He doesn't even know me," she said, stamping her foot angrily. "Why did he call me a floozy?"

"Lawman made a lucky guess," O'Shea sneered. "Just shut your mouth. We've got more important matters to take care of than your feelings gettin' hurt."

"*Nothing* is more important than a lady's feelings," the Gunsmith declared.

"Thank you, Clint," Sandra purred. "Nice to see there are still a few gentlemen left in this world."

"Listen, Adams," O'Shea began. "This was all a misunderstanding. We're new to these parts, and we sort of jumped to conclusions. Know what I mean?"

"Maybe I should march you fellas over to the sheriff's office and have you arrested for assault and battery," Clint mused.

"Sounds like the lawman don't like you much, Adams," O'Shea replied. "Look, I figured you for a bounty man. Well, if you was, you'd just kill us right here and now. Like I said, it was all a misunderstanding. We'll forget about if you will."

"And maybe you fellas will decide to get even with me for turning the tables on you."

"Nothing to get even for," O'Shea insisted. "You was just gettin' even for what we done to you. My boys roughed you up a little. You roughed them up a little, too. That makes everybody even.''

"Thrasher said he's going to kill me," Clint reminded the Chicago hoodlum.

"Thrasher works for me," O'Shea replied. "He'll do as I tell him. He won't kill anybody without my permission.''

"How about it, Thrasher?" Clint asked the boxer.

"I . . . I won't kill you, Adams," the pugilist replied.

"That's nice," the Gunsmith said as he slipped the brass knuckles over his left fingers. "All right. You can turn around now.''

Thrasher turned away from the wall to face Clint. The Gunsmith swung a left hook to the boxer's jaw, putting his weight behind the punch. The knuckle dusters slammed into his flesh hard. The blow sent Thrasher tumbling into O'Shea and Crusher.

The Gunsmith quickly removed the brass knucks and pocketed them while O'Shea and Crusher struggled to keep Thrasher from falling to the floor. The three hoodlums stared at Clint, astonished that he had hit the pugilist hard enough to knock him down.

Clint was surprised too. Thrasher was dazed and blood oozed from the corner of his mouth, but the boxer was still conscious. Crusher had previously absorbed enough punishment to render an ordinary man senseless, too. O'Shea had certainly hired a couple of tough sons of bitches.

"I guess that makes us even, Thrasher," the Gunsmith declared as he returned his modified Colt to the holster on his hip. "Now, why don't you fellas go upstairs to your rooms?''

"What about our guns?" O'Shea asked.

"You can come down to the front desk and pick them up later," Clint replied.

He waited until the three men mounted the stairs. Sandra smiled at the Gunsmith and treated him to a big wink before she hurried up the stairs to join the others. The Gunsmith turned to the desk clerk.

"Still have a room available, fella?" he asked.

"You sure you want to stay in this hotel with those three under the same roof?" the clerk inquired.

"Don't see I have much choice about that," Clint replied.

"You'd better watch out for those jaspers," the clerk warned. "You ain't gonna be real popular with 'em, you know."

"Yeah," the Gunsmith agreed, "I guess not."

SIX

Clint Adams decided to have a good dinner before he settled into his room and began trying to drum up business for his gunsmith trade. It would also give O'Shea and his men some time to cool off. Of course, they might decide to teach the Gunsmith a lethal lesson, but they'd probably wait a couple days for an ideal opportunity to strike without witnesses present. Probably arrange an "accident" for Clint.

The Gunsmith didn't intend to stay in Ten Pines that long. The town wasn't large enough to have a big population so there wouldn't be enough business to merit staying for more than twenty-four hours.

Clint left the hotel to find the sky full of drifting snowflakes. He hoped it was just another light flurry as he walked along the plankwalk, searching for a restaurant. He didn't have to look too hard. There was a sign advertising HOME COOKING on the third building down from the hotel.

The Gunsmith entered the restaurant. It was a pleasant place, neat and clean with checkered table cloths and quaint bric-a-brac on the shelves and window sills. There were only two customers eating: an obese man dressed in black sitting across from a dapper fellow clad in a three-piece suit.

"Good afternoon, sir," a woman's voice greeted Adams cheerfully. "Table for one?"

The speaker was an attractive young lady with raven black hair worn pulled back and braided. A wide, friendly smile shone from her well-scrubbed oval face. Her blue gingham dress was simple and practical. Clint appreciated the woman's hour-glass figure.

"Yes, ma'am," the Gunsmith said, doffing his stetson. "I'm by myself."

"Please, follow me," she invited.

"Anywhere," he whispered under his breath.

The waitress led Clint to a table in the middle of the room. He asked if he could have another table, selecting one closer to a wall. The woman agreed and escorted him to the position he had chosen.

"Lilly," the man in the suit called out, "Father Flynn and I are about to leave."

"Yes, sir," the waitress replied as she hurried to their table.

The Gunsmith watched the two men rise from their chairs. The man in the suit paid Lilly. Clint noticed the man carried a Remington revolver in a cross-draw holster. His wedge-shaped face was framed by a thick mane of gray hair. Although a toothy smile filled his mouth, his eyes remained cold and hard.

The fat man in black didn't bother to smile. Clint hadn't noticed the white clerical collar around the fellow's neck until then. The priest ignored the waitress and nodded his thanks to the other man. Lilly returned to Clint's table after the two men left.

"Have you decided what you'd like, sir?" the woman inquired.

"I'd like you to quit calling me 'sir'," the Gunsmith said with a grin. "My name is Clint. I really prefer to be called that. Especially by somebody as pretty as you.''

"Thanks for the compliment, Clint," Lilly replied with a smile. "Don't hear too many of 'em workin' here.''

"You'll hear some more from me," he assured her. "I'll have steak and potatoes, please.''

"Coffee?" she asked, jotting down his order on a note pad.

"Sounds good," Clint nodded.

"Comin' right up," Lilly said, heading for the kitchen.

The Gunsmith relaxed, leaning his chair firmly against the wall. A large object moved across the windows outside. Clint rose to get a better look. The object proved to be a buckboard with a canvas cover.

He watched the wagon roll toward the general store across the street. A figure dressed in a capelike garment drove the rig. The driver looked almost sinister, head and face concealed by a cowl. The Gunsmith crossed the room to the window, his curiosity whetted.

The wagon stopped at the store. Sheriff Connors approached the rig and said something to the mysterious driver. Clint wished he could read lips, unable to hear what the lawman said. The Gunsmith was surprised to see Connors touch the brim of his stetson. It was too cold to doff his hat.

"Something interestin' going on out there?" Lilly asked as she returned from the kitchen with Clint's coffee.

"Interesting maybe," Clint replied. "But I don't think it's apt to be very exciting.''

He watched Connors help the driver down from the wagon. The sheriff followed the hooded figure to the rear of the rig. They removed a panel and pulled two broad planks from the wagon.

"Must be Harlan Marshall's sister," Lilly commented, joining the Gunsmith at the window. "She inherited the general store after Harlan died. That was quite a blow to the town. Mr. Marshall was one of the founding fathers."

"I don't reckon Marshall signed the Declaration of Independence," Clint remarked. "So I assume you mean the founding fathers of this town."

"Right," the waitress confirmed. "Folks around here really admire the men who built this community."

The Gunsmith watched Sheriff Connors and the hooded driver set up a ramp by leaning the boards against the rear of the wagon. Connors climbed into the rig and rolled a third figure down the boards. Seated in a wheelchair, the individual was bundled in a blanket. Gray locks protruded from beneath a shawl wrapped around the invalid's head.

"That must be Harlan's sister," Lilly said. "I wonder if the driver will stay on to take care of her? He's probably a relation."

"*She's* probably a relation," Clint corrected. "The driver is a woman."

"How can you tell?" Lilly asked, gazing at the hooded figure.

"I can tell by the way the sheriff acted toward her," the Gunsmith answered.

"I suppose it makes more sense for one woman to take care of another," Lilly sighed. "But I wouldn't mind if there were a few more young men around Ten Pines."

"What about young Kirby, the veterinarian?" Clint

asked. "He looks about your age, twenty or so, and he seems to be well-educated. . . ."

Lilly laughed. "Do you like Joe Kirby?"

"I can't rightly judge him," the Gunsmith answered. "Only met the fella once."

"Come on, Clint," she insisted. "Did you like him?"

"Well," he shrugged. "Not really."

"You've got good taste," Lilly said dryly. "Joe Kirby is a conceited, snot-nosed kid. His pa spoiled him. Kirby comes in here once in a while. He likes to try to brush a hand against me—unless he has his wife with him."

"Oh," the Gunsmith began. "Reckon Kirby isn't a good fella to get mixed up with."

"By the way, Clint," Lilly said, "Are you married?"

"No," he replied. "But I'm not the type to settle down and raise a family anyway. I'm a traveling gunsmith. Tomorrow I'll be traveling onto someplace else."

"Figures," Lilly sighed. "Nobody stays on in Ten Pines except the founding fathers and their kin. A lot of the younger folks left when they were old enough to run off."

"Who exactly are these honored founders?" Clint asked. "If Marshall was the first one to die, there must still be a few left alive."

"You met two of 'em today," Lilly answered. "They were just in here."

"That sour-faced priest and that dandy with eyes like a rattlesnake?" Clint inquired.

"Father Flynn and Mayor Colby," the woman

stated. "They're two of the most respected men in town. Colby is definitely the richest fella in Ten Pines—at least he comes closer to being rich than anybody else does here. Colby owns the hotel, the saloon, and this place. He's also part owner of the livery. Probably figured he'd take over the general store too after Marshall died. Old Harlan's will cheated him out of that conquest."

"Sounds like Colby comes pretty close to owning this entire town," the Gunsmith mused.

"That's about the size of it," Lilly confirmed. "But most folks don't mind much. After all Colby and Matt Connors pretty much led the others when this town was built. I reckon that's why they're still the mayor and sheriff, ten years later."

"The sheriff, the mayor, a priest, and an old fella who ran a general store," Clint mused. "Who are the rest of the founders?"

"Doc Kirby, Joe's father," the woman replied. "That's all of 'em. The five men who built a town. What they don't own, they control. Colby has two sons. Edward runs the hotel and Sherman runs this restaurant, but their daddy is the real boss. Of course, you met Joe Kirby and you know his father is the town doctor. I understand he used to be a real good doctor, too."

"Used to be?" the Gunsmith asked.

"He drinks too much," she answered.

"I'll try not to get sick while I'm in town," Clint remarked. "Well, I reckon this little community has more character than I thought."

"You might say that," Lilly agreed. "I'll go see if your dinner is ready, Clint."

"Thanks, Lilly," he said with a smile. "And thanks

for the conversation, too. Folks haven't been real friendly toward me since I arrived in Ten Pines.''

"I'm just sorry you'll only be here for one day,'' she confessed.

"I'm almost sorry about that myself,'' the Gunsmith replied.

SEVEN

Clint Adams had often found business for his gunsmith trade in saloons. Men relax, drink, and spend money carelessly. They are easily convinced they need goods and services which they might not even consider while sober.

The Gunsmith had entered the Ten Pines saloon for this reason. However, there were only four customers in the bar. Three old men sat at a table playing checkers and sipping beer. Joe Kirby, the veterinarian, stood at the bar, drinking red-eye whiskey. Clint knew there was no point in talking to Kirby about firearms. He wandered over to the old timers instead.

"Any of you fellas interested in guns?" Clint asked. "A man's life can depend on how well his weapon performs in an emergency. A weak or worn mainspring or rusted cylinder can render a pistol useless."

"Don't own a pistol," one of the old men said, never looking up from the checkerboard to face Clint.

"Rifles can have problems, too," the Gunsmith declared. "And they can be improved. I can alter the trigger pull or adjust the sights for better accuracy."

"Don't own a gun period, Sonny," the old timer remarked. "Used to a long time ago, but not anymore. Any of you fellas own a gun?"

"Sold mine about a year ago," another ancient fellow replied. "How about you, Clem?"

"Hell," the third man snorted. "What do we need guns for? This is Ten Pines, not Dodge City. Ain't got killers and gunfighters runnin' around here. Besides, takin' care of trouble is what we have a sheriff for."

"Matt does a right fine job, too," the first man added, bobbing his head as if trying to convince himself of what he said.

"You fellas have a nice game," Clint said as he headed back to the bar.

"No one interested in your instruments of death, Mr. Adams?" Joe Kirby asked, his voice slightly slurred.

"Why don't you just stick a bottle in your mouth and be a nice, quiet drunk, Kirby?" the Gunsmith replied sourly.

"Men like you sicken me, Adams," Kirby replied dully. "You participate in murder, yet you feel no guilt."

"The hell with you," Clint muttered as he moved further down the bar.

"A decent man can . . . can make mistakes," Kirby insisted. "But he feels badly about it. Guilt is a human emotion. Animals don't feel guilt."

"Maybe they don't do anything to feel guilty about," Clint said dryly.

"That's what you are, Adams," Kirby accused. "You're an animal. But I'd never treat a beast like you. I'd never raise a finger to help a monster who peddles death for a living."

"That just about breaks my heart," Clint sighed. "Hey, bartender?"

"I hear you, friend," the man behind the counter replied. "What would you like to drink?"

"I'll have a beer," Clint answered.

"Sure," the bartender said. "Uh, try to ignore Joe. He's drunk and out of his head, you know."

"I met him when he was sober, and he won't get my vote in a popularity contest either way," the Gunsmith commented.

"Yeah," the bartender sighed as he placed a beer mug in front of Clint. "But you see, the kid's father is . . ."

"I know," Clint said, rolling his eyes toward the ceiling. "His father is one of the five men who built this town. Sorry, that doesn't impress me a helluva lot."

"Nobody has a conscience anymore," Kirby muttered in a drunken stupor as he stumbled toward the door. "Nobody cares about what happened. . . ."

Kirby almost staggered into Richard O'Shea and his two muscle-bound bodyguards as the trio entered the saloon. Crusher seized Kirby's shirt front and hauled the veterinarian across the threshold into the bitter cold.

"You goddamn barbarians." Kirby spat angrily.

Thrasher rammed a hard uppercut to the young man's stomach, Kirby fell to his knees and vomited on the plankwalk.

"Reckon they don't know who his father is," Clint commented to the bartender.

Richard O'Shea approached the Gunsmith, a wide smile plastered across his broad face. Thrasher and Crusher followed. Neither bodyguard tired to look friendly. The leader of the hoodlums leaned against the bar and folded his hands on his flabby chest.

"Hello, Adams," O'Shea greeted. "Good to see you again. Can I buy you a drink?"

"Already got one, thanks," the Gunsmith replied, holding the beer in his left hand. His right hovered near the Colt revolver on his hip.

"Mind if we join you?" O'Shea inquired.

"I thought we'd settled things, fella," Clint said. "What do you want now?"

"Just want to talk," O'Shea answered. "Besides, a friend of yours just arrived. Thought you might like to chew the fat together." He turned toward the door. "Come on in, Frank."

Frank Cameron entered the saloon. The tall, slender gunman brushed snow off his ankle-length cattleman's coat. He nodded at the Gunsmith as he approached the bar.

"Didn't expect to see you in Ten Pines, Clint," Cameron remarked, unbuttoning his coat to reveal the gunbelt strapped around his lean waist. A .44 Smith & Wesson was holstered on his hip.

"Didn't know you were headed this way either, Frank," the Gunsmith replied. "You working for O'Shea?"

"That's right," the gunfighter confirmed. "I understand you and these fellas had a misunderstandin' earlier today."

"I hope O'Shea doesn't want you to gun me down because of that nonsense," the Gunsmith said. "That would be a mighty dumb reason for one of us to get killed."

"Why don't we sit down and talk about this, Clint?" O'Shea urged. "You don't mind if I call you Clint, do you?"

"You've already done it twice," the Gunsmith shrugged. "Reckon it didn't hurt too much."

"You might want to hear what Mr. O'Shea has to say," Cameron suggested. "Only take a minute."

"All right," Clint agreed a bit reluctantly. "We'll sit over there."

The Gunsmith moved to the table he selected. He took the chair closest to the wall and sat with his back to it. Cameron looked a bit envious, but he settled into another chair, obviously a little uncomfortable because he couldn't shield his back. O'Shea, Thrasher, and Crusher joined them.

"Do any of you gents want anything to drink?" the bartender asked.

"Bring a bottle of whiskey," O'Shea ordered. "The best you've got. Irish whiskey if it's in stock."

"Yessir," the bartender replied. "How many glasses?"

"How many people are sitting at this table, you moron?" Thrasher snapped.

"I'll stick with my beer," Clint declared.

"I'll have beer, too," Cameron added.

"All right," the bartender said. "Then you'll want three glasses for the whiskey and two beers."

"How about that?" Thrasher snorted. "The moron can count."

"Let's get down to business," O'Shea urged, taking out a cigar. "I was impressed by how you handled yourself today. You're clever and slippery as a wet eel. You're also tough and you don't panic."

"He ain't so tough," Thrasher snorted. "He hit me when I wasn't expectin' it."

"Shut up, Thrasher," O'Shea snapped. "I'm tryin' to talk."

The bartender brought their drinks. The men waited until he returned to the bar before they continued the discussion.

"Look, Clint," O'Shea began, "I'm new to this part of the country. Thrasher and Crusher are damn good, but they're also from Chicago. The West ain't our natural environment, you might say. That's why I hired Frank here. He knows how things work out here."

"Sounds to me like you've got everything you'll need," Clint shrugged. "What do you want me for?"

"Because Frank tells me you're supposed to be one of the fastest guns in the world," O'Shea stated. "You and Frank are probably the best gunfighters in the West. I want you *both* on my payroll."

"Sorry," the Gunsmith answered. "I'm self-employed, and I plan to stay that way, fella."

"How much money do you make as a travelin' gunsmith?" O'Shea asked. "A thousand dollars a year? Can't be more than two thousand."

"Some years are better than others," Clint said.

"I'm prepared to offer you four thousand dollars," the Chicago hoodlum announced. "Four thousand dollars for one year in my employ. How's that sound?"

"Sounds like a lot of money," the Gunsmith admitted. "But I'm still not interested."

"There might be a chance to make more money, too," O'Shea added. "You see, I made some enemies back in Chicago. You ever hear of the Black Hand?"

"I've heard stories about it," Clint nodded. "The Black Hand is supposed to be some sort of secret society made up of Sicilian criminals."

"The Black Hand has been in this country since 1875," O'Shea declared. "It's always stayed pretty much in the Italian districts, but it's getting bigger. The Sicilians are already beginning to expand into the Irish sections of Chicago.''

"And the Black Hand drafted you into their organization?'' Clint raised his eyebrows. "But you're not on good terms with them so you left Illinois and headed West.''

"That's about it,'' O'Shea admitted. "The dagos might come after me. If that happens, I'll need somebody to take care of those bastards. If you kill a man who was sent after me, I'll pay an additional bonus of five hundred dollars.''

"I'm still not interested,'' Clint said as he finished his beer. "I might not get rich as a traveling gunsmith, but I think I prefer to work for myself.''

"You scared of the dagos, Adams?'' Thrasher sneered.

"I get in enough trouble without getting involved with a bunch of hoodlums,'' the Gunsmith replied. "I'm not going to lose any sleep worrying about your opinion of me, Thrasher.''

"Your decision, Adams,'' O'Shea sighed. "Sorry we can't do business together.''

"You'll get over it,'' Clint assured him as he rose from the chair.

EIGHT

The Gunsmith returned to the hotel. He stamped snow off his boots and removed his stetson to shake the clinging flakes from the hat. The owl-faced desk clerk recognized Clint Adams and nervously began to fidget with some papers on his counter.

"Oh, Mr. Adams?" he said. "Lilly, the waitress from the restaurant, claimed you left your pocket watch in the restaurant today. She brought it here to return to you."

"My watch?" Clint frowned as he reached into a pocket and removed his turnip watch. "I've got it right here."

"Oh, dear," the clerk began, his brow wrinkling with worry. "Well, I'm afraid I gave Lilly a passkey in order to let herself into your room to return the watch. Now it turns out the watch must belong to someone else."

"What the hell did you let her in my room for?" the Gunsmith asked angrily. "Is that your idea of security for your customers' belongings?"

"Oh, I'm certain Lilly won't steal anything," the desk clerk said, dabbing his sweaty brow with a handkerchief. "My brother has always said the woman is honest and a good waitress."

"So you must be Edward Colby," the Gunsmith mused, "the mayor's son."

"Oh, yes," the desk clerk said with a sigh. "But I'm afraid I'm not very much like my father. Not easy living up to his image of greatness."

"I guess not," Clint replied, although he had yet to see anything in Ten Pines which hinted of "greatness."

"I'm sorry about letting that woman upstairs," Edward told Clint. "But she should be coming downstairs any second now."

"I'll take care of this," the Gunsmith said. "Just be careful who you let into my room from now on."

Clint mounted the stairs. He hadn't even entered his room yet, and he had to check the tag on his key to be certain which room was his. He found a door with the same number tacked on its top panel as the number on his key.

The Gunsmith unlocked the door. His hand dropped to the holstered Colt as he opened the door and entered.

Lilly waited inside the room. She had decided to make herself comfortable. The woman lay on the bed, a blanket drawn up to her throat. Lilly's blue gingham dress was draped over the back of a chair.

"Hello, Clint," she greeted with a sly smile. "I saw you from the window, so I figured I'd just relax and wait for you."

"Well, I'm here now," the Gunsmith said. "By the way, the pocket watch doesn't belong to me."

"I know it doesn't," Lilly replied as she pushed down the blanket to reveal her large, firm breasts. "But it was the only excuse I could think of."

"Excuses," Clint mused, closing the door. "Funny how a man and a woman feel a need for each other, but they still come up with excuses.''

''You feel a need for me, Clint?'' the woman asked.

''Let me show you how much,'' the Gunsmith stated as he began to strip off his shirt.

He undressed quickly. Naked, Clint walked to the bed and hung his gunbelt on the headboard. He slid into the bed beside Lilly and took her in his arms. Their mouths crushed together, tongues probing eagerly. Lilly's fingernails moved along the curve of his back.

Clint began to kiss her soft neck while his hands found her breasts, stroking and fondling them tenderly. Her nipples became rigid under his skillful touch. His lips moved down her throat, slowly. Lilly moaned with pleasure while Clint lowered his mouth to her breasts.

He kissed the soft mounds of flesh and tongued her nipples. Clint's hands slid down her body to her thighs. He stroked Lilly's warm, sensitive flesh and gradually moved his fingers to the center of her womanhood.

Lilly raked her nails across his back. Clint's hands moved faster. The woman groaned as the fires of passion increased within her. Clint suddenly broke the embrace and straddled her torso. He placed his rigid penis between her breasts, gently pressing them together. He moved his hard manhood slowly within the tunnel of soft flesh.

The woman groaned. Clint shifted his body and slid himself down her torso, his stiff cock slithering across her belly. Lilly's hands found his member and steered it to her womb.

He entered her. The woman arched her back to receive him, but Clint wasn't one to rush love making. He worked himself back and forth within Lilly, increasing the tempo as she approached her peak.

Lilly convulsed in an orgasm, her body thrashing

beneath him. She cried out with joy and hugged Clint, her legs locked around his hips. The Gunsmith held his load and slowly began to rotate his penis by grinding his loins against Lilly's delicious body.

He thrust again and again, faster, harder, and deeper. The woman gasped. Her nails bit into his shoulder as she neared a second summit. Clint pumped his fleshy shaft into her with all his might. Lilly exploded in another passionate tremor. Only then did the Gunsmith climax as well, firing his seed deep within her womb.

"God," Lilly whispered, "that was wonderful."

"You're wonderful," he told her, kissing the woman's lips. "Tell me, Lilly, you're not from Ten Pines originally. Why do you stay in a town which doesn't seem too agreeable to you?"

"I'm just trying to save up enough money to move on to California in the spring," Lilly replied. "Plan to go to San Francisco. Have you ever been there, Clint?"

"Yes," the Gunsmith said. "I've been there quite a few times. It's a terrific city. Exciting and full of activity."

"Sounds lovely," she sighed.

"It is," Clint assured her. "You'll fit in perfectly."

"Maybe we'll meet again there some day," Lilly mused.

"Maybe," the Gunsmith agreed. "But we're together here and now tonight."

NINE

Lilly left the room before Clint Adams awoke the following morning. The only evidence of her visit was the indentation in the mattress beside the Gunsmith.

Clint climbed out of bed and pulled on his clothes. He buckled the gunbelt around his waist and headed for the window to see how much snow had fallen during the night. The Gunsmith groaned when he saw the thick carpet of white which covered the ground below. The snow was still coming down and it didn't look like it was going to stop either.

He slipped on his sheepskin jacket and gloves before he left the room and descended the stairs. Edward Colby wasn't at the front desk. Clint had already paid for his room in advance, so he could simply leave the key at the desk. However, the Gunsmith decided to hitch up his team to the wagon and get Duke ready to travel, then he'd turn in the key.

Snow formed large drifts which all but covered the plankwalk. Clint's boot skidded on ice. He braced himself along the wall and slowly made his way along the planks. The wind howled like an arctic demon. Half-frozen snow pelted the Gunsmith, stinging his exposed flesh. He turned up his collar and pulled down the brim of his stetson for protection.

Clint could barely see through the relentless flurry. Buildings became great shadows without definite shape. Half-blind, the Gunsmith groped his way to the livery stable, wading through ankle-deep snow.

He reached the livery and pulled open the door. Clint slipped inside, grateful to find shelter from the snowstorm. He doffed his hat and used it to brush off snow from his jacket. Christ, what a mess, Clint thought. He wondered if it would be wiser to leave Ten Pines now before the weather got worse or to wait to see if the blizzard would subside completely later on.

A strange figure stumbled away from some stalls at the opposite side of the livery. Dressed in a long, tattered coat, the man was doubled up as he stumbled toward the Gunsmith. A large hump strained the fabric between the stranger's shoulder blades. He smelled as if he washed his clothes in rot-gut whiskey.

"Oh, shit," the man muttered in a slurred voice. "Don't beat me. I just come here to get outta the snow is all."

"Don't worry, fella," Clint assured him. "I won't hurt you, but the liveryman might take exception to you staying here."

"Oh," the shabby fellow raised his head weakly. A dense black beard covered his jaw and a wool scarf was bound around his head. His nose was large and hooked like an eagle's beak.

"You have a place to go, fella?" Clint inquired.

"Oh, sure," the man replied, squinting his eyes into narrow slits. "I'll be goin' now. God bless ye, neighbor."

He pushed open the door and stumbled outside. The Gunsmith pulled the door shut and sighed sadly. Town drunks are a miserable sight. They kill themselves one bottle at a time.

Suddenly, Clint noticed a nervous neigh. It was

Duke. Something had disturbed the big black gelding. The Gunsmith drew his modified Colt revolver and slowly moved toward Duke's stall.

"Easy, boy," Clint called softly. "Don't fret so. Everything is all right, big fella."

The Gunsmith doubted the truth of this statement. The last time he heard Duke utter such a neigh of distress, Clint had found a dead man's body.* He trusted Duke's judgment. Something was very wrong and that usually meant danger.

Clint approached Duke's stall. The Arabian's head thrashed up and down as he neighed his warning. The Gunsmith glanced about, seeking any possible threat. Then he saw what upset the gelding.

Strapped to the rails of another stall was a gruesome, bloodied figure. Although the body's face had been destroyed by the blade of a knife and his features bathed in blood, the Gunsmith was pretty sure the corpse had once been Joe Kirby.

Kirby's arms were tied to the rails. A burlap gag was jammed in his teeth. Flesh had been peeled from his cheeks and his nose had been sliced off. Both eyeballs had been punctured by the tip of a blade.

"Jesus," the Gunsmith rasped, feeling his stomach convulse.

He forced himself to lean closer to examine the dead man more closely. Kirby's shirt was soaked with blood. The hostler's throat had been cut from one ear to the other. Clint stood up and stepped back from the corpse.

"Well," the Gunsmith remarked, "he sure as hell didn't commit suicide."

_____

*The Gunsmith #9: Heavyweight Gun

TEN

"Oh, my God," Sheriff Matt Connors whispered when he examined the mutilated corpse. "I ain't seen a man chopped up this bad since the time I was in the Dakota Territory during a Sioux uprisin'."

"It's pretty bad," Clint agreed. "But I think Kirby was dead before the killer chopped him up."

"What makes you say that?" the lawman asked, raising an eyebrow suspiciously.

"A lot of blood appears to have gushed out of his slit throat," the Gunsmith explained. "But there isn't much blood from those slashes on his face. When a man is dead, his heart stops pumping blood. That means the only blood left is what's still in his veins and arteries, which isn't a lot. Hell, I'm not a doctor, but I figure Kirby wasn't tortured. Somebody mutilated his corpse. Probably to put a good scare in the rest of us."

"For Joe's sake, I hope you're right," the sheriff commented. "But why would somebody want to do this? I've known Joe since he was knee-high to a chicken. Can't say as he was ever real popular, but he never had no enemies neither."

"Somebody didn't like him much," Clint mused. "Maybe his father or his wife knows something."

"And maybe you do, Adams," Connors remarked dryly.

"If I killed Kirby," Clint began. "Why did I come to your office and tell you his body was lying over here? Why didn't I just leave town the way I planned to?"

"Could be your way of trying to throw me off," the sheriff replied.

"What about the man I saw when I came into the livery?" Clint asked.

"A bearded hunchback?" Connors shrugged. "I've lived in this town ever since I helped build it ten years ago. I've never seen a hunchback—drunk or sober—in this town."

"He smelled of whiskey," the Gunsmith said. "But maybe he wasn't drunk. He might have pretended to be drunk."

"We ain't got no hunchbacks in Ten Pines," Connors declared. "But we've got some mighty suspicious strangers in town all of a sudden. Those fellas from Chicago aren't choirboys. Neither are you, Adams."

"Aren't you the least bit suspicious of Frank Cameron?" Clint inquired. "I didn't think his reputation was any better than mine."

"Cameron is in town?" Connors frowned. "When did he show up here?"

"Met him in the saloon last night," the Gunsmith answered. "He's working for Richard O'Shea."

"So the hootowl from Chicago has hired a Western gunman as well as two pet gorillas," the sheriff commented. "Well, I can sort of lump them together as a single suspect, but you're still more likely than they are."

"Any idea what motive I might have for killing Joe Kirby?"

"If I did," Connors began, "you'd be in a jail cell right now."

"Well," Clint sighed, "while you're trying to figure out what reason I might have for killing a fella I hardly knew, don't forget to check on the other folks in Ten Pines because one of them did it."

"Yeah," the lawman snorted, "a drunken hunchback."

"Maybe the hunchback is a drifter who wandered into town," Clint mused. "In this weather he'd have to find shelter."

"Why would this hunchbacked drifter kill Joe?" Connors asked, obviously doubting the theory had a single grain of truth.

"Maybe he's loco," Clint said. "Maybe he didn't kill Kirby, but he might have overheard something which will be a clue to the identity of the killer. I don't know anything for sure except I saw the son of a bitch."

"Where'd he go?" the sheriff asked.

"Outside," the Gunsmith answered. "Maybe we can follow his tracks in the snow."

"If we can find a hunchback in this town, I'll be happy to consider him a prime suspect," Connors agreed.

They emerged from the livery. The icy wind still lashed out with frosty fury at the two men. Clint gazed down at the snow-covered ground. The blanket of white was monotonously featureless. The Gunsmith could hardly see the bootprints he and the sheriff had made in the snow when they'd walked from the sheriff's office to the livery.

"Goddamn snow drifts have covered the bastard's tracks," the Gunsmith remarked through chattering teeth.

"I hear that happens a lot when you're trying to follow the tracks of an imaginary hunchback," Connors commented dryly.

"Sheriff," Clint insisted, "our tracks are almost invisible now. "It's no wonder the hunchback didn't leave a trail."

"Bullshit," Connors sneered. "Maybe you're the one that's loco."

"That hunchback won't be able to hide very easily," the Gunsmith declared. "Folks are bound to take notice of him."

"You planning to search the town for this boogieman?" the sheriff inquired.

"If I can find him, will you consider the possibility my story is true?" Clint asked, trying to peer through the snow to see if anyone might be watching from a window.

"I'll even apologize," the sheriff assured him.

"Then I can hardly wait to find him," Clint declared.

"All right, Adams," the sheriff sighed. "I figure this is going to upset the whole town no matter how I handle it, so I'll go along with you while we search for this phantom hunchback."

"Fine with me, Sheriff," the Gunsmith assured him. "When we find him, just remember what Joe Kirby looked like. If the hunchback is our killer, he's one dangerous son of a bitch."

"I'll remember," Connors said. "Ain't likely I'm

going to forget what I saw back in that livery. Reckon I'll see it often enough in my nightmares.''

"That'll make two of us,'' Clint admitted.

ELEVEN

The Gunsmith and Sheriff Connors started the search at the logical point by checking the closest building first—the general store. Clint approached the door from the side in order to use the frame for cover if necessary. Connors noticed Clint's right hand hovered near the grips of his Colt as his left moved to the door knob.

"Aren't you jumping to conclusions, Adams?" the lawman asked. "You don't know the killer is in there."

"You don't know he isn't," the Gunsmith replied as he eased the door open.

The general store was drab and dusty with a limited stock of canned goods, beef jerky, flour, and tools. However, there was nothing drab about the pretty brunette behind the counter. The woman smiled as the Gunsmith entered the store.

"Our first customer," she greeted, her pale green eyes glowing, "and an attractive man at that."

"Thanks, ma'am," Clint replied. "May I say you look a lot better without that hood covering your face."

"Oh?" she raised an eyebrow. "You must have seen us arrive yesterday. "My aunt and I are new here. Are you a resident of Ten Pines, or are you just passing through?"

"I'll be here for a little while longer," the Gunsmith replied. "My name is Clint Adams, Miss . . ."

"Melissa Marshall," the woman answered. She noticed Connors had entered the store behind Clint. "Hello, Sheriff. Nice to see you again."

"Afraid this ain't a social visit, ma'am," the lawman declared.

"Oh?" Melissa frowned. "Is something wrong?"

"We're looking for a man," Clint explained. "A bearded fellow with a hunchback."

"What has this man done?" she asked. "Is he some sort of criminal?"

"Adams claims to have seen the fella," Connors stated. "He may not even exist, but if he does, we have to have a talk with him. Understand?"

"Do I understand that you're looking for someone who might not exist?" The woman shook her head. "Not really."

"I don't understand either," the sheriff said lamely. "But we're still lookin' for this hunchback."

"Well," Melissa sighed, "you won't find anyone like that here. My aunt Edith and I are the only people in the place. No one except you two has even been in the store yet. I'd certainly remember a bearded hunchback."

"I'm sure you would, Miss Marshall," Connors nodded. "Come on, Adams. We've wasted enough of the lady's time."

"Is there another entrance to this building?" Clint asked. "The hunchback might have entered through a back door."

"There's a door in the rear," Melissa confirmed. "But that's to the house. You see, half of this building is a store and half is a house. Aunt Edith is back there.

She's resting, and I don't like to disturb her. She's an invalid, you know.''

"Don't worry about disturbing me, Melissa," a reedy voice declared. "I've already been listening to this story. It's an interesting tale even if it doesn't make any sense."

A frail figure in a wheelchair sat at the threshold of a doorway leading to another section of the building. Clad in a black cotton dress with a blanket across her lap and a shawl wrapped around her throat and head, Edith Marshall looked miserable.

Clint wondered if Melissa was adopted. She certainly did not resemble her aunt. The younger woman had a perfectly shaped oval face with a cute button nose and wide, appealing lips. Edith's face was lean with heavily powdered, hollow cheeks. A pair of smoked glasses were perched on the bridge of her hawkish nose.

"Good morning, ma'am," Connors greeted. "Sorry to bother you, but we're lookin' for a feller."

"There's no hunchback in here, Sheriff," Edith stated. "But you're welcome to take a look—providin' you don't mess up my house."

"Thank you, ma'am," Clint said. "We'll check real quick, just in case the fella sneaked in."

"Just make it quick, don't light any lamps which aren't already lit," Edith instructed, "and don't turn up the flames of any that are. My eyes are sensitive to light."

"Yes, ma'am," the sheriff replied. "Come on, Adams. Let's get this over with."

Edith rolled her chair backward to make room for the two men. Clint and Connors entered the house section. The sweet scent of jasmine assaulted their nostrils. The odor was almost overwhelming. Two large incense burners produced twin billows of the scented smoke. The old woman's sense of smell must have been in worse shape than her eyes.

The first room was a parlor with cozy settee and matching armchairs. A walnut-and-brass clock ticked loudly from its perch on the fireplace mantle. Clint and the lawman walked across the large throw rug in the middle of the room and inspected the kitchen.

The room was neat and clean. The wooden floor had recently been mopped and droplets of water dribbled from the muzzle of a pump attached to the sink. The back door was securely locked and bolted. The sheriff tried the doorknob and sighed.

"Nobody busted in here, Adams," Connors stated. "I think we've bothered these ladies enough. Don't you?"

"Let's just take a peek at their bedrooms to be sure," the Gunsmith urged.

"This sort of thing ain't gonna make us popular with folks," the lawman muttered. "I gotta live in this town, Adams,"

"If you don't find the killer of Joe Kirby, you'll be pretty unpopular, too, Sheriff," Clint reminded him.

"I ain't so sure I ain't lookin' at him right now," Connors said, glaring at the Gunsmith.

Clint didn't argue with the lawman. He and Connors left the kitchen and quickly peered into the women's rooms. Edith and Melissa had separate bedrooms. Clint guessed the bedroom with a large oakwood chest at the foot of the bed probably belonged to Edith. The other room appeared to be Melissa's. Two steamer trunks stood on end and open to serve as closets.

The Gunsmith approached the trunks and rifled

through clothes hanging inside the luggage. Clint's hand rested on the grips of his revolver in case an assailant was hidden inside the trunk. This may have seemed an unlikely place for a killer to lurk, but the Gunsmith had once come close to fatal attack by an opponent who used such a tactic.*

"Jesus, Adams," Connors snapped. "This has gone far enough."

"All right," Clint agreed. "Let's go."

"I trust you gentlemen have satisfied your curiosity," Edith remarked. She sat in front of the fireplace, back turned to the men as she stared at the blazing logs.

"Yes, ma'am," Connors replied. "Sorry to disturb you, ma'am."

"That's all right," Edith answered. "I hope you find your mysterious felon—whoever he is."

Clint and Connors left the house section. Melissa waited in the store. The men apologized to her as well. Melissa simply smiled in response, her pale green eyes trained on the Gunsmith.

"After you find your hunchback," she began, "come back and I'll show you some of my goods, Clint."

"Sounds like a great deal," the Gunsmith replied, trying to keep his eyes from straying to her breasts. "I'll look forward to it."

---

*The Gunsmith #15: Bandit Gold

TWELVE

The saloon wasn't open yet. Clint and Sheriff Connors checked the front of the building to be certain it was locked up, then they circled around the building to the rear. Harry, the bartender, had a room in the back. After pounding on the door for a while, the Gunsmith and Connors managed to wake up Harry.

"What the hell is goin' on, Matt?" Harry demanded as he appeared at the door, dressed in his red flannel underwear and armed with a Greener 12-gauge shotgun. "Oh, howdy, Clint."

"We're lookin' for a hunchback feller with a beard," the sheriff answered. "He might have killed Joe Kirby."

"What?" Harry blinked with surprise. "You tellin' me Joe's dead?"

"Cut up like a Christmas turkey," the lawman confirmed.

"Damn a dog's ass," Harry rasped. "Joe was my best customer, too."

"We're searchin' every place in town tryin' to find the bastard," Connors explained.

"And you want volunteers to help?" the bartender inquired. "Sure, I'll help."

"We want to search your place to be sure the jasper ain't here," the lawman interrupted.

71

" 'Course he ain't here," Harry declared. "How could he get into my place without me knowin' it?"

"Just let us have a quick look around, all right?" Connors insisted.

"Sure," Harry shrugged. "I ain't got nothin' to hide. Come on in."

The Gunsmith and Connors entered the bartender's quarters. Harry's room was small and untidy, dirty clothing on the floor and tattered blankets bundled on the bed. Clint noticed a pair of boots by the foot of the bed. A puddle of water had formed around the footgear.

"You been out for a stroll, Harry?" the Gunsmith inquired as he examined the boots.

"Stepped outside to pee," Harry answered nervously.

"Wearing just your long-johns?" the Gunsmith asked.

"I pulled on a coat before I went outside," the bartender replied. "Hey, you're not suggesting that I'm protecting this hunchback you're lookin' for?"

"Ain't suggestin' nothin', Harry," the sheriff assured him. "Let's look over the barroom, Adams."

The Gunsmith and Connors moved to the saloon. They checked behind the bar and inside the stockroom. There was no one hidden in either area. Clint and the sheriff apologized for bothering Harry. The bartender took the disturbance in stride and wished them good hunting.

Clint and the lawman checked the hotel next. Edward Colby was on duty at the front desk. He was quite willing to assist them in the search for the hunchback murder suspect. Edward seemed very distressed by Joe's death—much more so than Sheriff Connors or Harry had been.

"Joe and I grew up in this town," Edward stated. "Most of the others who were born here left. His death is sort of like losing a piece of my own past."

"Mind if we check the rooms upstairs?" the Gunsmith asked.

"No," Edward assured him, "of course not. Although I've only got ten rooms and only three of them are occupied, since you left, Mr. Adams."

"I figure I might be back," Clint replied. "I take it O'Shea and his crew have the three rooms?"

"Oh, yes," Edward nodded nervously. "Mr. O'Shea and that woman of his aren't married, so I insisted they get separate rooms. The other two gentlemen are sharing a room right next to Mr. O'Shea."

"Let's pay them a visit," Connors declared. "Better not push too hard, Adams. I suspect those Chicago boys can play rough if they have to."

"So can Frank Cameron," the Gunsmith commented. "If he doesn't have a room with the rest of O'Shea's men—then where is that gunhawk holed up?"

"I don't know, Adams," the lawman said. "But I don't like havin' a gunfighter in Ten Pines, period. If you're cleared of murder, I hope you'll leave as soon as possible."

"Cleared of murder?" Edward gulped loudly. "You mean Mr. Adams is a suspect, yet he's helping you hunt for this hunchback?"

"Sort of a funny arrangement," Connors admitted. "But if it works, who cares?"

"I don't understand," Edward said in a puzzled voice.

"You're lucky," Connors snorted. "You don't have to. I'm the one who has to try to figure out what he's doing. Hell, come on, Adams. This is gettin' embarrassin'.''

Clint followed Connors up the stairs. They located O'Shea's room and prepared to knock on the door. Clint heard the faint creak of hinges. He turned sharply, hand snatching the modified Colt from leather in a swift, smooth motion. Frank Cameron stood in the doorway of another room, his Smith & Wesson revolver in his fist.

''Looks like we got ourselves a Mexican stand-off here, Clint,'' Cameron commented, his voice as steady as the hand which held his pistol.

''Not really,'' the Gunsmith replied calmly. ''You're holding a single-action revolver. That means you have to cock the hammer before you squeeze the trigger. My gun is a double-action, self-cocking revolver. All I have to do is squeeze the trigger.''

''Won't make much difference,'' Cameron said. ''I always cock the hammer and squeeze the trigger at the same time anyway.''

''It'll make a difference,'' Clint stated. ''Only a split second, but that's enough and you know it, Frank.''

''Wouldn't make no difference at all if we quick draw,'' Cameron remarked.

''But we're not going to quick draw, Frank,'' Clint smiled, ''because you haven't been paid to.''

''Then let's put our guns away and you fellers can tell me what you want with O'Shea,'' Cameron suggested.

''Fair enough,'' the Gunsmith agreed, slowly lowering his Colt.

Cameron lowered his pistol. Both men holstered their weapons. Sheriff Connors sighed with relief and rapped his knuckles on the door to O'Shea's room. Sandra answered the door. The blonde was dressed in a frilly pink nightgown. She ignored the sheriff and greeted Clint with a wide smile.

"Hello, Clint," Sandra said. "Fancy seeing you here."

"Life is just full of surprises," the Gunsmith replied. He frowned when he noticed a dark bruise on her cheek. "You and O'Shea having some problems getting along?"

"Something like that," she admitted. Sandra turned to Connors. "Why's the sheriff here?"

"Have to speak to Mr. O'Shea, ma'am," Connors stated. "Ain't this his room?"

"Did Richard sign the register and write this room number down as the one he'd be in?" Sandra demanded.

"Well," Connors shrugged. "I reckon he did."

"That goddamn Irish rattlesnake!" Sandra exclaimed.

She marched to another door and began pounding her fists on it. Clint turned to Cameron.

"How come your name isn't in the register?" the Gunsmith inquired.

"I arrived late last night," the gunfighter replied. "Desk clerk wasn't on duty. So I just let myself into a room."

"How'd you unlock the door?" the sheriff wanted to know.

"Jimmied the latch with my knife," Cameron answered. "O'Shea will pay for my room. No problem, Sheriff."

"That's breakin' and enterin', feller," the lawman declared sternly.

"You thinkin' of arrestin' me?" Cameron inquired, his eyes narrowed. "Better not try it, lawman. I ain't goin' to no jail."

"Is that a threat?" Connors demanded.

"You're not goin' to take me in," Cameron stated simply.

Before the sheriff could reply, Richard O'Shea opened the door which Sandra had been pounding on. He stared at the Gunsmith and Sheriff Connors with surprise.

"What the hell do you—" he began.

Sandra suddenly swung a right cross to O'Shea's jaw. He fell back against the doorjam, startled by her actions. Clint noticed the Irishman was already sporting a black eye. He guessed Sandra wasn't the type of woman to accept being slapped around without hitting back.

"Jesus," O'Shea rasped, "what got into you now?"

"You signed the register with your name for the room you stuck me in, you polecat bastard!" Sandra snapped angrily.

"Hell," he replied, rubbing his jaw. "That was just a mistake, honey . . ."

"Mistake!" she fumed. "You done that on purpose so anybody lookin' for you would come to my room instead. You don't care if they kill me, so long as your precious hide will be safe!"

"You got it all wrong, honey," O'Shea began lamely.

The woman kicked him in the shin. O'Shea grunted and hopped on his good leg. Sandra clipped him on the jaw with another solid right. He fell against the door hard.

"Don't you just love a woman with spunk?" the Gunsmith commented with amusement.

Sandra stomped angrily back to her room, entered, and slammed the door. O'Shea pushed himself away from the door to his room and scowled as he spat a globlet of blood on the floor.

"Want me to shoot her, Mr. O'Shea?" Cameron asked dryly.

"Shit," the Irishman muttered. He turned his attention to Clint and the lawman. "What do you two want?"

"Want to search your rooms," Connors explained. "We're lookin' for a feller what might've murdered a local resident here in town."

"Search my room?" O'Shea growled. "What for? I ain't done nothin'. You figure I got this killer hid under my bed, Sheriff?"

"We got a problem, Mr. O'Shea?" Thrasher inquired as he opened another door and emerged from his room. A Police Colt was thrust in his belt.

"Takin' care of trouble is what you pay us for," Crusher added as he joined the boxer in the hallway.

"Ah, hell," Clint sighed. "Looks like there's going to be some killing again. I hate killing folks this early in the morning. Kind of puts a damper on my whole day."

"I got a cure for that, Clint," Cameron warned, his hand close to the grips of his Smith & Wesson.

"Everybody calm down," O'Shea urged. "The sheriff wants to see if we got a killer hidden in one of our rooms."

"I'm a killer," Cameron said casually. "But I haven't had no call to kill nobody lately. Especially not some liveryman in a one-horse town like this."

"How did you know the liverman was killed?" Clint asked.

"I seen you and the sheriff leave the livery together when I looked out the window a while back," the gunfighter answered. "Seemed logical."

"Seems like mighty skinny evidence to make up a statement like that," the sheriff said.

"I'm good at guessin' about things," Cameron said with a shrug.

"Save it for the next state fair," O'Shea said crossly. "What's this killer supposed to look like?"

"We don't know for sure he's a killer, but he's supposed to be a hunchback with a beard," Connors answered. "At least, that's how Clint described the jasper."

"Oh?" O'Shea raised his eyebrows. "So you seen this feller, Adams?"

"That's right," the Gunsmith sighed. "Mind if we look now?"

"I ain't hidin' any hunchbacks," O'Shea laughed. "Go ahead and look, but don't mess with my luggage or go through my stuff in those drawers. Don't like people messin' around in my private stuff."

The Gunsmith and Sheriff Connors checked in O'Shea's room. No one was hidden in the closet or under the bed. Clint wondered what O'Shea had in his big steamer trunk and cloth suitcase, but he didn't figure there was a hunchback hidden in either article of luggage.

They also searched Cameron's room. The gunfighter sat by his saddlebags on the bed, guarding them from the investigators. However, there was no one hidden in his room either. Crusher and Thrasher also agreed to let their quarters be searched. Still no clues as to the whereabouts of the mysterious stranger Clint had encountered.

"Sandra," O'Shea called to his mistress as he rapped lightly on her door. "You want 'a open up and let these fella's check for that hunchback they're huntin' for?"

"Hell no!" she shouted angrily. "I ain't openin' this door so you can come bargin' in here looking at my personal things."

"Never mind, Mr. O'Shea," Connors told the Irishman. "We'll be movin' on now. Thanks for your cooperation."

The lawman and Clint Adams started for the stairs. The Gunsmith stopped abruptly and gestured for the sheriff to do likewise.

"What is it now, Adams?" Connors asked with exasperation.

"I was just thinking," Clint began. "If Cameron could sneak in and get a room without signing the register, maybe somebody else could, too."

"You want to check every room in this hotel?" the sheriff rolled his eyes with frustration. "I'm gettin' a mite tired of this, Adams."

"You want to find Kirby's killer or not?" the Gunsmith replied simply.

"All right, Adams," Connors groaned. "We'll search the rest of the hotel. But if we don't find somethin' pretty soon, you're gonna be sorry you ever rode into this town."

"I'm already sorry," Clint muttered sourly.

THIRTEEN

"This is blasphemy, Sheriff!" Father Flynn declared, his eyes bulging angrily from his chubby face. "Blasphemy to come seeking a murderer in the House of God!"

"Father," Connors began as he and the Gunsmith spoke with the priest at the threshold of the only church in Ten Pines. "We're not accusin' you of hiding the feller. We just want to make certain he ain't here and you don't know it."

"I don't like men coming into my church wearing guns," Flynn told them.

"You want to take the chance of encountering a murderer without a gun, Father?" Clint asked. "I saw how Joe Kirby was cut up. I don't like the idea of taking on a knife artist by tossing salt on his tail."

"Very well," the priest said tensely. "You may enter, but don't draw your guns unless you find this maniac. And watch your language."

"Yes, sir," the sheriff agreed. "We'll be real respectful."

Connors and Clint Adams walked up the aisle, glancing at the pews to be certain no one was crouched among them. They moved to the priest's chambers behind the altar.

"Nobody in here neither," the sheriff said as he peeked inside the priest's chamber. "Any other bright ideas, Adams?"

"The confessionals," Clint replied as he headed for the two closet-like doors separated by an ornate screen.

"Come on, Adams," Connors groaned. "Nobody could be hiding there."

"Don't touch that, you blasphemous heathen!" Father Flynn snapped.

Clint opened a confessional door. A man fearfully cowered against a corner of the chamber, burying his face in a fur hat. The Gunsmith grabbed his arm and hauled the man out of the confessional. A pale round face with spectacles perched on a nose discolored by broken blood vessels stared back at the Gunsmith.

"Don't . . . don't hurt me, mister," the man urged, his breath reeking of cheap whiskey. "I'll leave. Uh, where am I?"

"Take your hands off that man!" Flynn ordered.

"Jesus Christ, Adams," Sheriff Connors snapped. "That's Doc Kirby, Joe's father. He ain't no goddamn killer."

"Sheriff!" Flynn gasped. "Your language is disgraceful, sir!"

"Sorry, Father," Connors replied with a shrug. "Did you know Doc was in that booth?"

"He was making a confession when he . . . well, fell asleep," Flynn explained. "Poor man is a drunkard, you know."

"Doc couldn't kill anybody," Connors told the Gunsmith. "He ain't no bearded hunchback neither."

"No," Clint replied. "He doesn't look at all like the man I saw at the livery."

"The livery?" Doc Kirby blinked dully. "My son works at the livery. He's a horse doctor, too. Well, I doctor people and he doctors animals. But, I done a terrible thing to my Joseph. Just a terrible awful thing."

The doctor began to cry. As he sobbed, he reached into a pocket and took out a flask of whiskey. Sheriff Connors stepped forward and caught his wrist before Kirby could raise the bottle to his lips.

"What do you mean, you done somethin' awful to Joe?" the lawman demanded.

"Sheriff," the priest began urgently.

"What the hell are you talkin' about, Doc?" Connors insisted, grabbing Kirby's lapels and shaking him forcibly. "Talk, damn it!"

"Matt?" the doctor said dully. "Why are you hurting me?"

"Joe's dead, you drunken idiot!" Connors snarled. "Somebody carved him up and killed him deader than a drumstick!"

"Joe's d-dead?" Kirby's eyes swelled behind the lenses of his wire-rimmed glasses.

"Did you kill him?" Connors demanded. "Do you know who done it? Talk or I'll—"

"Sheriff," Clint Adams said tensely, "if you don't quit using your spurs on that man, I might just decide to show you how it feels."

Connors released Kirby and slowly turned to stare at the Gunsmith, astonished by Clint's threat. The Gunsmith met his stare without blinking. The lawman gazed at Clint's hard, brown eyes for almost five seconds, then he quickly looked away.

"Joe's dead," Kirby whispered, desperately gulping from his bottle. "I knew somethin' like this was gonna happen someday. The sin was bound to catch up with us."

"Calm down, Doc," the sheriff told him.

"The sin of this town," Kirby continued. "The curse was bound to happen."

"What's he talking about?" Clint asked.

"He's crazy drunk," Connors replied gruffly.

"So many sins," Kirby sobbed. "Father, help me. I've gotta make a confession. The sin is heavy on my soul."

"Of course, my son," Flynn replied.

"But my son is dead," Kirby said sadly. "He must be buried. Did he die without last rites? Oh, God. No one should die in this town without last rites. Our souls are already in enough danger."

"Father," Connors said sharply, "I reckon you'd better take care of him. Come on, Adams. Let's leave this man to deal with his grief."

"Sure," Clint agreed. "I want to talk to you anyway."

FOURTEEN

"All right, Sheriff," the Gunsmith began when they emerged from the church. "What was that all about?"

"What was what about?" Connors asked, turning up his collar to shield himself from the icy wind which still fired snowflakes like buckshot pellets.

"The sin of this town?" Clint asked. "What's that mean?"

"Doc's drunk, damn it," Connors replied. "You listen to every big mouth drunk what starts to blabber and bawl?"

"He also said he knew something like this was going to happen someday," Clint insisted. "You were about to beat the tar out of him when he said he'd done something awful to his son."

"At first I thought he was confessin' to the murder," Connors shrugged. "Then I realized he was just rantin'. Goddamn drunks rant all the time. They see snakes under their beds and bats in their closets."

"Matt!" a figure bundled up in a long tweed coat and a rabbit fur hat called to the lawman. "Matt, I want to have a word with you."

"Ain't I popular today," the sheriff muttered.

Clint recognized the man as he drew closer. It was Mayor Colby. The sheriff nodded a greeting, but the

85

mayor didn't seem to be in a very sociable mood.

"What the hell do you think you're doing, Matt?" Colby snapped. "Joe Kirby has been killed and you're wandering all over town with the chief suspect and the two of you are searching everybody's business and home, looking for some hunchback!"

"We haven't searched your house yet, mayor," Clint commented dryly.

"Who the hell are you, young man?" the mayor demanded.

"His name is Clint Adams," Connors answered. "He's better known as the Gunsmith. Ever hear of him?"

"Some sort of gunfighter, isn't he?" Colby frowned.

"Hey, fella," Clint said sharply. "Don't talk about me as if I'm not here. I'm right in front of you."

"Why isn't he in a jail cell?" Colby asked the sheriff. "Why haven't you arrested him?"

"Unless you've got a town ordinance against finding a dead body and reporting it to the sheriff," Clint stated, "I haven't committed any crime."

"We're gonna freeze out here," Connors declared. "Let's head over to Sherman's place and get some coffee. We can at least be warm while we argue."

No one objected to the lawman's idea. The Gunsmith, Sheriff Connors, and Mayor Colby entered the restaurant and moved to a table. Lilly waited on them. She seemed less cheerful than when Clint had met her the day before. Apparently, she too had heard about the murder of Joe Kirby.

"You gentlemen care for breakfast?" Lilly asked.

"Just coffee," Colby replied.

"I'll have some breakfast," the Gunsmith declared.

"Eggs, ham and toasted bread sounds just fine, Lilly."

"I'll get the coffee right away," she said. "Your breakfast will take about twenty minutes, Clint."

"That'll be fine," the Gunsmith assured her.

Lilly headed for the kitchen. Colby glared at Clint.

"Better enjoy your breakfast because it may be the last meal you'll ever have outside of a jail cell," the mayor hissed.

"Colby," Clint sighed, "why don't you shut your mouth long enough for somebody else to talk?"

"You're a stranger in this town, Adams," Colby began.

"Thank God for that," Clint muttered. "I'd hate to live here."

"Maybe you'll get to die here," Colby mused. "We haven't had a hanging in this town for a long time."

"With or without a trial?" the Gunsmith inquired.

The mayor stiffened, and he looked to Sheriff Connors for help. The lawman had removed his stetson and nervously fingered the brim as he gazed down at the table.

"Let's all calm down a bit," he said at last. "Adams, you tell the mayor what you told me."

The Gunsmith explained how he had found Joe Kirby's body and his brief encounter with the hunchback. Mayor Colby frowned.

"You believe him, Matt?" the mayor asked.

"Ain't sure one way or the other," Connors shrugged. "But I don't rightly know why Adams would murder Joe that way. Then again, I can't figure why anybody would want to kill him."

"When I was in the saloon last night," Clint began, "Kirby was pretty drunk. Mouthed off to me about being a gunsmith, and how I'm peddling death. Didn't bother me really because I'm just passing through, and I don't get mad that easy.''

"Is that a fact?'' Colby sneered.

"My point is,'' Clint continued, "Joe Kirby might have riled up a lot of people when he was drunk. Did he ever do anything that would have got somebody mad enough to want to kill him?''

"Hell, no,'' Connors answered. "Joe didn't have any guts even when he was drunk. Never got too nasty. Every so often somebody would hit him in the mouth, and he'd just go home and sleep it off.''

"I heard he cheated on his wife,'' Clint commented.

"Did you also hear that his wife left him four days ago?'' Connors answered. "Little tart took off for Carsontown or Grundyville. Ain't seen hide nor hair of her since.''

"Wait a minute,'' Colby began. "Adams said he saw a bearded hunchback, not a woman. Besides, no female could kill a man that way.''

"You'd be surprised what some women can do,'' Clint remarked. "And, I can't say for sure that the hunchback killed Joe Kirby. He smelled of whiskey. He may have just been sleeping off a drunk in a stall and didn't have anything to do with the murder.''

"Pretty unlikely anybody could sleep through a murder,'' Colby commented.

"If the fella was drunk enough he could sleep through a full-scale battle with cannon fire,'' Connors corrected. "But that doesn't explain how the jasper just vanished.''

"Maybe he isn't in Ten Pines anymore,'' Colby suggested. "Could be some crazy old hermit who staggered into town and back out again.''

"He'd have to be mighty crazy to wander into that

snow blizzard," Clint replied. "I reckon that's possible, but it sure isn't probable. Did you ever hear any rumors that Kirby had anything valuable hidden at the livery or maybe at his house?"

"Hell, no," Connors snorted. "Joe ran the livery and was a half-ass horse doctor. You figure a fella like that would have a fortune tucked away?"

"Rumors pop up about old hermits and elderly spinsters having a mattress full of money or a barrel of gold hidden under the floorboards of their house," Clint replied.

"Never heard any talk like that about Joe," the sheriff stated. "Besides, Joe never set foot outside of Ten Pines. Everybody in town knows everything about everybody else."

"No rumors about Doc having a treasure either," Mayor Colby stated before Clint could make that suggestion.

"Well," Clint sighed, "I can't think of any other possible motive—unless Doc Kirby's talk about the 'sin of this town' means something."

Mayor Colby stiffened again. "Doc's a drunken old fool, Adams. Don't put any stock in his nonsense."

"What's he mean by the 'sin of this town'?" the Gunsmith insisted. "Don't tell me it's nothing because you fellas are getting too hot under the collar for me to believe that."

"Doc's wife run out on him because he drinks too much," Connors said sharply. "Doc tends to blame everybody else for that. You know how drunks never figure anything is their fault."

"Seems like a lot of wives have left their husbands in Ten Pines," Clint mused.

"Joe was a drunk just like his father," Connors

stated. "Come to think of it, that's probably what Doc meant when he said he'd done 'a terrible thing' to his son. Probably blames himself for his son's drinkin' problem."

"Maybe," Clint nodded. "A doctor named Benjamin Rush back in 1807 claimed alcoholism is a disease which might be handed down from one generation to another. Still, that might explain Doc's remark, and Joe's drunkenness might explain why his wife left him. But I seem to recall you saying your wife ran out on you too, Sheriff."

"My wife was a goddamn tramp, Adams," Connors snorted. "The fact that two-cent whore run out on me doesn't have diddly-damn to do with Joe's murder."

"I'd say the most likely suspect is you, Adams," Colby commented grimly.

"Any idea what motive I might have?" Clint asked dryly.

"You're a gunfighter," the mayor accused, "a killer. Maybe you enjoy killing people."

"That's ridiculous," the Gunsmith replied. "Whoever murdered Kirby is still running around loose. You'd better concentrate on finding him and quit trying to blame me for a crime I didn't commit."

"Lilly!" the mayor called out.

"Yes, sir, Mr. Colby?" the waitress said, hurrying to their table.

"Is my son here?" he demanded.

"You mean Sherman?" Lilly asked.

"Sherman runs this damn place," Colby nodded. "I sure as hell don't mean that spineless disappointment Edward who cowers behind his desk all day."

"Sherman is here, sir," Lilly told him.

"Go fetch him and tell him to bring his gun," Colby instructed. "We've got a killer to arrest."

"Hold on a minute," Connors began.

"You're afraid of this gunfighter's reputation," the mayor snapped. "That's why you haven't arrested him."

"We don't have any evidence," the sheriff said.

"There isn't any hunchback in town either," Colby declared. "I don't want Adams to just ride out of town when he might be a murderer."

"Don't worry about that," the Gunsmith commented as he gazed at the falling snow outside the window. "I won't be going anywhere for a while."

"And what do you plan to do while you're staying in Ten Pines?" Colby asked.

"I reckon I'll try to find a killer," the Gunsmith replied. "But first, I plan to have breakfast."

FIFTEEN

Clint Adams returned to the livery to check on his animals and property. Joe Kirby's ghastly corpse had been removed. Only a crusty brown stain of dried blood marked where the dead man had been.

The Gunsmith searched the livery, hoping to find some evidence to either identify the killer or prove that the bearded hunchback wasn't just a figment of his imagination. However, he failed to find a single scrap of cloth, clear bootprint or anything else to help his personal investigation.

"I sure wish you could talk, big fella," Clint told Duke.

The big black gelding uttered a soft snort, almost a sigh, as if to say, "I can just do so much."

"Yeah," the Gunsmith agreed. "Guess I'm gonna have to handle this mystery on my own."

Clint shuffled through the snow. It was almost knee-deep. More snow was still coming down, faster and harder than ever. He mounted the plankwalk, stamping snow from his boots. Clint didn't realize he was in front of the general store until the door opened. Melissa's lovely face appeared, smiling at the Gunsmith.

"You look cold, Clint," she remarked. "Come in

93

and have a cup of coffee with a bit of brandy in it to help insulate you from the chill.''

"That's the best offer I've heard all day," Clint replied.

He entered the store. Melissa moved to a potbellied stove and took a blue tin coffee pot from its hot iron top. She poured the steaming black liquid into two cups and placed them on the counter.

"Watch your fingers," she warned. "Coffee's hot."

"Yes, ma'am," he replied.

"Please call me Melissa," the woman urged, taking a bottle of brandy from under the counter.

"This is mighty kind of you, Melissa," Clint said.

"Well, we're both strangers in town," she stated, "so we've got something in common. I imagine you find this town a bit lonesome, too."

"A bit," he confessed. "But I'm used to spending a lot of time on the trail away from people."

"Being lonely depends more on who you're with than how many people are around you."

"That's a fact," Clint agreed. "I reckon you feel a bit out of your element here in Ten Pines."

"You might say that," Melissa admitted, uncorking the bottle. "Say when."

"When," the Gunsmith told her after she poured a few drops of brandy into his coffee. "Where are you and your aunt from? Philadelphia?"

"You're close," she replied. "Pittsburgh."

"A long way to travel just to run a general store."

"My aunt is all the family I have," Melissa shrugged. "I couldn't let her come out here alone."

"How long have you been taking care of her?"

"For the last four years," the woman replied, pouring some brandy in her coffee as well. "Since she was crippled by a fall down a flight of stairs. Spinal damage. She'll be in that wheelchair for the rest of her life."

"I'm surprised she decided to move out West," Clint commented. "Elderly folks tend to get set in their ways and like to stay in one place."

"Aunt Edith is an unusual old lady," Melissa told him. "She's always wanted to come out West, and she didn't want to die in the filthy slum which her old neighborhood had become. The East is becoming a very unsavory place, Clint."

"It's been a long time since I've been east of the Mississippi," the Gunsmith said. "Maybe that's just as well."

"Have you found your murderer yet, Clint?" Melissa inquired, sipping her coffee.

"Not yet," Clint confessed. "The mayor thinks I did it, and the sheriff isn't real sure I'm innocent."

"Are you?" the woman asked with a smile.

"If you have any doubts," Clint answered, "you really shouldn't have invited me inside."

"I trust you, Clint," she assured him. "Call it woman's intuition, but I'm sure you never killed anyone. I can see that in your eyes."

"Better look again," the Gunsmith told her. "Fact is, I've killed quite a few men in self-defense, but I never murdered anyone."

"That's what I meant, of course," Melissa stated. "Your eyes are strong, noble, and brave. There isn't any glint of a murderer in them."

"Sure wish some of the other folks in town agreed with you," Clint sighed. "Maybe you should take a look at everybody else's eyes in Ten Pines. Maybe you wouldn't find a murderer, but I suspect there's more than one liar around here.''

"Everybody lies, Clint," Melissa declared. "It's just a matter of how much and why."

"Reckon that's true," the Gunsmith agreed as he finished his coffee. "Much obliged, Melissa. Now, I'd better be on my way."

"Stop by anytime," she urged. "It's been a pleasure."

"The feeling's mutual," he grinned.

Clint spent most of the afternoon asking questions. Vainly, he sought someone who may have seen the bearded man with the humped spine stagger from the livery that morning. Nobody had seen or heard a damn thing. It was as if the hunchback had melted into the snow and disappeared.

The Gunsmith returned to the hotel at sundown. He mounted the stairs and walked to his room. Cautiously entering, he checked his quarters. Satisfied that the room was empty, Clint inspected his gear. His clothing hadn't been disturbed. He checked his saddlebags and found the New Line Colt was still there. Clint unwrapped the small .22-caliber pistol and made certain it was in perfect working order.

Clint loaded the cylinder of the New Line Colt and returned it to his saddlebags. The situation in Ten Pines had become risky enough to merit carrying the little gun for backup. The Gunsmith decided to get some sleep to ease some of the tension in his muscles and mind. Maybe some rest would clear the Gunsmith's brain so he could unravel the mystery—or at least figure out what he should do next.

Clint drifted into a shallow sleep. Long ago, the

Gunsmith had learned how to rest his muscles, nerves, and mind without shutting down his senses. Clint's senses remained alert as he slept, like a great cat, forever wary of danger.

The Gunsmith slept for three hours. His slumber was rudely interrupted by an earth-shaking explosion. Clint awoke abruptly, automatically grabbing his .45 Colt from the holster hung at the headpost of his bed. The building still trembled as if rocked by an earthquake.

"Jesus," Clint rasped as he rolled off the mattress.

The Gunsmith was still fully dressed. He had only removed his gunbelt and boots before he had stretched out on the bed. Voices cried out in alarm and fear. Clint smelled smoke somewhere within the hotel. He hastily pulled on his boots and hurried from the room.

Smoke and plaster dust billowed through the hallway. Clint pointed his pistol at a pair of burly figures which staggered through the fog, coughing violently. The Gunsmith held his fire when he recognized Thrasher and Crusher.

"What happened?" Clint shouted his question.

"Somethin' blew up," one of the muscle men rasped.

"Brilliant deduction," the Gunsmith muttered.

"Clint?" Frank Cameron called as he poked his head out of O'Shea's room, his Smith & Wesson revolver in his fist. "Any idea what the hell happened?"

"Somethin' blew up," Clint answered dryly. "Where's the smoke coming from?"

"Down the hall," Cameron gesturing with his revolver. "I've gotta look after my meal ticket. If you want'a play hero and go check it out, be my guest."

The Gunsmith hurried through the corridor, his Colt

held ready. A loose board shifted under his boot, nearly throwing Clint off balance. He stepped around the unsteady footing and fell against a wall. The smoke was more dense now. Clint could barely see. His nostrils filled with dust and grime.

Clint groped forward, squinting his eyes, trying to peer through the thick, dark cloud of dirty smoke. Yellow light flickered. Clint approached the flames carefully. Another floorboard gave way under Clint's weight. His boot broke through the wood. He hastily pulled it free and braced his back against the wall.

Then he saw the outline of a doorway. It had been chewed and battered by the blast. Flames danced along the ragged entrance. The room within was a shambles of rubble. Snow blew in through a shattered window only to disappear in the ovenlike heat inside the room.

The Gunsmith felt something soft under his boot. Clint glanced down. Three fingers protruded from underneath his boot. The Gunsmith quickly moved his boot and stared at the bloodied stump of severed hand covered with dust.

SIXTEEN

The citizens of Ten Pines formed a line along the staircase and handed buckets of half-frozen water up to the burning room. Clint Adams, Richard O'Shea's two bodyguards, and Frank Cameron assisted in fighting the fire. Half an hour later, it was under control.

Men attacked the remaining flames with wet blankets, smothering the last of the blaze. Sheriff Connors dug at the rubble. As he expected, a mangled, almost shredded corpse lay beneath the debris.

"My God," the lawman rasped, staggering from the room. "Edward Colby's under there. Christ, he's a mess."

"Edward's dead?" a tall, well-built young man among the firefighters, cried out. "You're telling me my brother has been murdered?"

"We don't know he's been murdered," Connors replied.

"How do you think he was blown to pieces?" Sherman Colby snapped. "Reckon he swallowed a keg of gunpowder and burped too hard?"

"Calm down, Sherman," the sheriff urged. "We'll find out what caused Edward's death."

"And how do you intend to do that, Sheriff?" Sherman demanded.

"I'm gonna start by talkin' to everybody who was in

the hotel when the explosion occurred,'' Connors replied. ''And the first thing I want'a know is who found the body?''

''You did, Sheriff,'' the Gunsmith reminded him. ''All I found was a severed hand in the hallway. You located the rest of him.''

''You seem to have a real knack for bein' around when a murder has been committed, Adams,'' Connors declared, glaring at the Gunsmith.

''Listen, fella,'' Clint began tensely. ''I wasn't the only person who was here when that explosion went off. Crusher and Thrasher were in the hall when I came out of my room. Frank Cameron was already in Richard O'Shea's room with a gun in his hand. Why don't you talk to them as well?''

''I intend to talk to all of you,'' the lawman announced. ''Down in the lobby. *Right now*!''

Sheriff Connors assembled Clint Adams, Richard O'Shea, Frank Cameron, Sandra, Thrasher, and Crusher in the small lobby of the Ten Pines hotel. Most of the townsfolk rubbernecked at the door and windows despite the bitter cold and snow outside. The sheriff insisted that the audience leave so he could talk freely with the roomful of suspects.

The Gunsmith spoke first, explaining precisely how the explosion woke him and how he discovered the others in the hall before moving to the room that contained the remnants of Edward Colby's crushed body. The sheriff turned to Thrasher and Crusher.

''So you two boys were in the hall when Adams came out of his room?'' the lawman asked.

''That's how he tells it,'' Crusher growled.

''What do you mean by that?'' Connors asked.

''We didn't see Adams open the door and come

out," Thrasher explained. "He just suddenly appeared among all that smoke with a gun in his hand."

"They were half-blind and choking on the smoke," Clint said. "It was pretty hard to see anything."

"What about you, Cameron?" Connors inquired.

"I heard the explosion and headed straight for my employer's room," the gunfighter answered. "My job is to look after the feller that hired me."

"How come you managed to get from your room to O'Shea's quarters before Adams was even in the hallway?" Connors wanted to know.

"If Clint's tellin' the truth," Cameron began, "he was in bed asleep. I was already awake when the explosion went off. Didn't waste time puttin' my boots on either."

"I figured there might be wood splinters and broken glass all over the place," Clint stated. "I wasn't about to step out of my room without boots. For all I knew, the stairs might be on fire."

"Besides," Cameron added with a wry grin, "I'm a bit younger than Clint. Can't expect his reflexes to be as good as mine."

"Thanks, Frank," the Gunsmith said dryly.

"Sure thing, Clint," Cameron smiled.

"Mr. Shea?" Connors began.

"O'Shea," the Irishman corrected, taking a box of matches from the pockets of his black-and-gold dressing gown. "I can't add anything to what Cameron has already told you, Sheriff."

"You didn't even set foot outside of your room to see what happened?"

"That's right," O'Shea confirmed as he struck a match and lit a cigar. "I hire other folks to do that sort of work for me."

"Uh, huh," the sheriff muttered. "Do you have anything to say, ma'am?"

"Not a thing," Sandra replied, holding a pink robe tightly around her body. "I stayed in my room and hoped the whole building wasn't about to come crashing down. What was I supposed to do, Sheriff? Run out there with a wash basin and pitcher yelling 'Where's the fire?' "

"In other words all of you were innocent bystanders," Connors sighed. "Too bad we got Edward's dead body upstairs, or we could just pretend it never happened."

"Hey, Adams," Thrasher chuckled. "You sure you didn't see a bearded hunchback creepin' around in the hall?"

"Nope," Clint replied. "All I saw was you and Crusher."

"You suggestin' we caused that explosion and set fire to the room afterward?" the boxer demanded.

"Nope," the Gunsmith assured him. "I'm just saying what I saw."

"Well," Connors commented, "I reckon we won't solve much tonight. You folks can all go back to bed. I'll continue my investigation in the morning. None of you better try to leave town. Especially you, Adams."

The sheriff marched from the hotel. The Gunsmith headed for the stairs, but O'Shea called his name sharply.

"You want something?" Clint asked, his hand resting on the butt of his revolver.

"I want to know what you're up to, Adams," O'Shea said gruffly.

"O'Shea," the Gunsmith began, "you and I don't

have any quarrel with each other. Do yourself a favor, and keep it that way.''

With that, Clint Adams mounted the stairs and headed for his room.

SEVENTEEN

The Gunsmith didn't feel much like going back to sleep. An unexplained murder less than ten yards from where he was staying had a way of ruining a good night's sleep. Clint stripped off his clothes and used a cloth in the wash basin to scrub down his body. He toweled his skin vigorously to keep the chill from his flesh.

The sound of knuckles rapping on the top panel of the door drew the Gunsmith's attention. He wrapped the towel around his loins, holding it in place with one hand and gathered up his .45 Colt with the other. Clint approached the door and stood clear of it as the knocking continued.

"Who is it?" he asked in a loud voice.

"It's Sandra, Clint," a woman's voice answered. "May I come in?"

"I don't have any clothes on," the Gunsmith replied.

"I don't care about that," she insisted. "I need to talk to you. Please?"

"Can't it wait until morning?" he asked, listening carefully, trying to determine if anyone was in the hall with Sandra.

"Come on, Clint," she said. "I don't bite. Honest."

"All right," he agreed, slowly turning the knob.

The Gunsmith opened the door cautiously and peered outside. Sandra smiled at him. She appeared to be alone, but Clint didn't drop his guard as he swung the door wide and ushered her inside.

"Are you always so nervous?" Sandra asked, glancing down at the gun in Clint's fist.

"That's how I stay alive," the Gunsmith answered.

Sandra closed the door. She scanned over Clint's body, clad only in the towel. The woman smiled and nodded.

"I like your . . . taste in clothes," she remarked.

"Glad you approve," Clint said dryly. "Now, what's on your mind?"

"I can't sleep," Sandra replied. "Thinking about what happened to that poor desk clerk upsets me. My God, they didn't even dig his body out from under all that rubble. He's still lying in that shambles of a room. Lying there, dead and mashed up like a bug somebody stepped on."

"Why don't you turn to Richard for comfort?" Clint asked. "He's your fella, isn't he?"

"Richard is never much comfort," Sandra commented. "He doesn't understand women. He doesn't care what upsets me."

"How did you get teamed up with him?" the Gunsmith inquired.

"Lock the door," she advised. "I don't want us to be disturbed."

"All right," Clint agreed, locking the door. "Now tell me about you and O'Shea."

"Well, I was poor and desperate when I met Richard back in Chicago about six months ago," Sandra answered. "He had money and style—or at least I thought so. See, I'm not much different from Frank Cameron and everybody else associated with Richard. He's my meal ticket.''

"Bringing you to Ten Pines doesn't seem to be a great favor," Clint stated.

"Richard doesn't do me any favors anymore," Sandra replied. "That ended when he got in trouble with the Italians back in Chicago. He dragged me out here, but when he finds another woman he wants, he'll dump me faster than a rotten egg.''

"Maybe you should dump him first," the Gunsmith suggested.

"But there's nobody else for me to go to instead," Sandra told him.

"Don't look for security from me," Clint warned her. "I'm not the family man sort. I'm a drifter. A traveling gunsmith without ties and no wish for any.''

"Who said anything about ties?" Sandra said. "What I want from you is a warm body and a little passion. A *lot* of passion if you have it in you.''

The Gunsmith replied by removing the towel. His maleness jutted out hard and fully erect. Sandra approached quickly. They embraced, their mouths meeting hungrily. Clint's hands slowly descended to caress Sandra's breasts which strained the flimsy fabric of her pink nightgown. He slipped the garment from her shoulders, and it slid down the length of Sandra's body to the floor.

Suddenly, the woman sank to her knees, her lips parted wide. She kissed the head of his penis. Clint sighed with pleasure as her mouth climbed the fleshy shaft of his manhood. Her tongue licked and caressed him. She took him fully into her mouth, lips reaching down to the root of his cock. Sandra cupped his balls in one hand as she rode her lips up and down the length of his swollen shaft.

The Gunsmith began to reach his brink. Sandra sensed this and took her lips from his rigid organ. She rose and marched purposefully to the bed. Clint Adams eagerly followed.

Sandra climbed onto the mattress, positioning herself on her hands and knees. Her naked buttocks were aimed at the Gunsmith as he joined her on the mattress. He knelt between her legs, gently stroking the soft flesh of her delightful round rump.

His hand slipped between her thighs and found the warm, moist center of her womanhood. Sandra moaned happily as Clint's fingers slid inside. He moved his hand back and forth. She rocked her body to the rhythm of his strokes.

The Gunsmith slipped his hand free and inserted his throbbing manhood into her womb. Sandra trembled with pleasure and wiggled her rump against his belly, working him deeper. Clint's hips moved slowly, assisting the penetration. His hands caressed her thighs and buttocks as he gradually increased the tempo of his thrusts.

Sandra groaned and moved faster. Clint rammed himself home again and again. Sandra's head shook violently as she tried not to cry out as an uncontrollable orgasm shook through her body with spasms of passion.

Clint stroked and fondled her, resisting the urge to plunge into her again until he too was satisfied. The Gunsmith continued until Sandra was ready, then he drove his throbbing cock faster and harder than before. Sandy yelped with delighted surprise, bucking her body wildly to receive his thrusts.

At last, Sandra reached her second climax. Clint gasped as his member finally exploded its seed deep within her womb. Sandra slumped to the mattress. Clint lay behind her, their bodies still linked together.

"God, Clint," Sandra whispered, "I feel better than I've felt for a long, long time."

"I enjoyed making love to you," Clint confessed. "But I sort of suspect O'Shea might have sent you to try to pump me for information."

"Oh, he did," she replied. "Richard thinks the Italians back in Chicago may have hired you to kill him. He figures the explosion might have been an unsuccessful attempt on his life."

"What do you think?" Clint asked.

"I think you're very good in bed and that's all I really care about," the woman answered. "But I don't figure you're a hired killer. I also think if you wanted Richard dead, he'd already be a corpse by now."

"O'Shea is wrong about me," Clint assured her, "and he's wrong if he thinks that explosion was meant for him. Whoever did it intended to kill only one man—Edward Colby."

"But why would anybody murder a meek little desk clerk," Sandra asked, "and blow up a whole room to do it?"

"I don't know," the Gunsmith admitted. "But I've got a hunch this is only the beginning."

"The beginning of what?" She seemed puzzled.

"A goddamn nightmare."

EIGHTEEN

Sandra left after making love to the Gunsmith. Clint slept soundly until dawn. He awoke feeling surprisingly relaxed for a man who was the prime suspect for two murders in Ten Pines.

He knew he hadn't murdered Joe Kirby or Edward Colby. He also knew he'd remain the number-one choice as murder suspect until the real killer was apprehended. Clint didn't have a hell of a lot of faith in Sheriff Connors' ability to solve this mystery, so the Gunsmith decided he'd better try a little harder to find the murderer.

Since he wouldn't be able to avoid the sheriff, Clint figured it was best to see him before Connors came looking for him with more outrageous accusations and thinly veiled threats. He headed straight for the sheriff's office. Connors seemed less than pleased to see him.

"Good morning, Sheriff," the Gunsmith announced. "How'd you sleep?"

"Not worth a damn," Connors snorted as he dragged himself from behind his desk. "What do you want, Adams?"

"I was about to offer to buy you breakfast," Clint shrugged. "But if you're going to be this disagreeable, I reckon I'll eat by myself."

"Ain't no reason why we can't be civil 'bout things," the sheriff commented. "Let's go have that breakfast."

The Gunsmith and Connors entered the restaurant. Lilly escorted them to a table and took their orders. Clint and the sheriff waited until she had disappeared inside the kitchen to get their coffee before either man spoke about the murders.

"Have you been able to come up with any hunches about either the Kirby killing or last night's murder yet, Sheriff?" the Gunsmith asked, glancing at the window. Snow was still coming down. It seemed like it would never stop.

"You got any idea who the killer is?" the sheriff asked dryly.

"I have some idea who it isn't," Clint answered.

"Naturally, you're not the killer," Connors sneered.

"Naturally," the Gunsmith nodded. "But I think we can disregard O'Shea and his people as well."

"We?" the sheriff raised his eyebrows. "You're gonna help me catch the killer?"

"That's right," Clint confirmed. "Somebody has to."

"Is that a fact?" Connors snorted. "Well, why do you say we can disregard O'Shea and his group?"

"Three reasons," Clint began. "First, Thrasher and Crusher were out in the hallway when I came out of my room to investigate the explosion."

"Seems to me that makes 'em more suspicious."

"If you lit a fuse to a stick of dynamite—and judging from the amount of damage done, I'd say the killer only used one stick—wouldn't you use a long fuse so you'd have enough time to get to cover? I don't figure hanging around in a hallway only a few yards from an explosion is much cover.''

"Dynamite could have blown up before they figured it would," the sheriff replied.

"That's possible," Clint allowed. "But last night Crusher asked who'd want to blow up the room and set a fire, as if these were two separate acts."

"That sounds suspicious, too."

"Right," the Gunsmith nodded. "It sounds suspicious, but the killer wouldn't have said something like that."

"Could have been a slip of the tongue," the sheriff said. "Those boys don't seem too smart, but they're mean enough to kill a total stranger."

"But the killer wouldn't have made a slip of the tongue about something that didn't happen."

"What the hell?" Connors glared at Clint.

"The dynamite explosion ignited a kerosene lamp in the room," Clint explained. "That's what caused the fire."

"And how can you be sure about that?" the sheriff stared hard at the Gunsmith.

"Because if the fire was started on purpose," Clint began, "the killer would have wanted Edward Colby's body to burn. You saw his corpse. Was it burned?"

"No," Connors admitted. "Mighty mangled but not burned."

"Finally, O'Shea thinks I'm the killer," Clint said with a shrug. "He's running from a pack of hoodlums—back in Chicago. He also thinks I might be working for them."

"Those are some mighty interestin' observations, Adams," Connors remarked. "Especially since proving O'Shea's people ain't involved makes you look even more suspicious.''

"Oh, yeah?" Clint asked. "Why?"

"Because these murders are obviously the work of a stranger in town," Connors stated. "Six strangers show up in Ten Pines and suddenly we got two murders in two days."

"*Eight* strangers in town," Clint corrected. "Don't forget Edith and Melissa Marshall. Nine, if you count the hunchback."

"Those two women couldn't be responsible for these murders—especially an old lady in a wheelchair," the sheriff declared. "And, you still ain't proved this hunchback of yours is real."

"I wouldn't dismiss any suspects if I were you, Sheriff," the Gunsmith told him.

"Including you?" Connors asked.

"If I was in your boots, I'd still be suspicious of me," Clint admitted.

"That's a mighty honest remark," the sheriff said. "Especially since you figure I can forget about O'Shea and his henchmen."

"I'll make one exception there," Clint declared. "Frank Cameron."

"The gunfighter?" Connors frowned. "Why is he more suspicious than the others?"

"Because he isn't from Chicago," Clint answered. "Cameron kills for money. Plain and simple. If somebody paid him enough, he might be willing to kill everybody in this town."

"Why would somebody pay him to kill Kirby and Colby?" the sheriff demanded.

"You tell me," Clint replied. "This is your town. Is there any reason anyone would want to terrorize the people here?"

"Terrorize, hell," Connors snorted. "You're coming up with some wild theories, but none of them make sense."

Lilly returned with the coffee. She apologized for taking so long. Clint assured her that was no problem. The waitress headed back to the kitchen.

"Have there ever been any stories about gold or silver in this area?" the Gunsmith asked.

"Christ, no," Connors growled. "Your loco ideas aren't helping to clear you, fella."

"Especially when you're not willing to listen," the Gunsmith replied sourly.

"What's that supposed—" the sheriff stopped short when he heard a bell chiming outside. "That sounds like the church bell. This ain't Sunday."

Clint rose from his chair and moved to the door. Through the blur of falling snow, the Gunsmith saw a cluster of people congregated in front of the church. He buttoned up his sheepskin jacket and left the restaurant, ignoring the sheriff's order for him to wait.

The Gunsmith headed for the church. Connors followed him, cursing angrily as he tried to catch up with the Gunsmith. Clint's long-legged stride quickly carried him to the church. He elbowed his way through the crowd to the entrance.

The doors of the church stood open. The citizens of Ten Pines stared in horror at the figure behind the altar. The Gunsmith entered the church and slowly approached the ghastly black shape lying on the marble floor.

Father Flynn was just below the crucifix face up, his arms spread wide apart. A spike had been hammered into his forehead.

NINETEEN

"My God," Sheriff Connors rasped as he stared up at the priest. "This is awful. What kind of a sick mind would do something like this?"

"Let's get him covered up," the Gunsmith suggested.

"Yeah," Connors agreed. The lawman turned to the crowd. "Don't just stand there gawkin'. Somebody get something to cover him up with for crissake."

"Yes, sir, Sheriff," Sherman Colby replied from the group. He hurried out.

"A lot of blood around his head," Clint noticed as he drew closer. "The blood is dry, too." He stepped behind the altar. "So are the patches of carpet where somebody scrubbed with some sort of lye soap and a hand-bristle brush. See how the threads were torn up by the brushing? Those patches are about two shades lighter than the rest of the carpet."

"What does that mean?" Connors asked, puzzled by Clint's observations.

"It probably means the killer scrubbed the floor to hide footprints," Clint explained. "Clever bastard isn't leaving anything to chance."

"Downright remarkable how you can figure all this stuff out, Adams," Connors growled. "But you still haven't come up with a single clue as to the identity of the killer except for that phantom hunchback of yours."

"Well, we know the killer is a very strong man," Clint stated. "The priest wasn't small." We also know the murderer is very clever, ruthless enough to kill, but cautious enough to avoid being seen or leave tell-tale evidence."

"Except the dead bodies we keep finding," Connors said dryly.

"The killer *wants* us to find the bodies," Clint said. "After all, the murderer clearly strikes at night. He could have easily dragged his victims out of town and left them in a snow drift. Instead, he makes each murder more shocking than the last."

"It'll be pretty hard for him to do much worse than murderin' a priest in his own church," the sheriff commented.

"I hope he doesn't come up with something worse," the Gunsmith mused. "Our killer is a shrewd son of a bitch with a macabre imagination."

"Well, Adams," Connors began. "You're a clever fella, and you seem to have a pretty good imagination. That drunken hunchback is proof of that."

"The hunchback is real, damn it," Clint insisted. "Although I'm not so sure he's still alive."

"What do you mean?" the sheriff asked.

"A man with a crooked spine couldn't have done this," Clint gestured at the priest. "At least, not by himself. That means either somebody in this town is hiding the hunchback, or he isn't around anymore. The killer may have figured the hunchback was a witness, killed the poor devil, and buried him in the snow."

"Why not use the hunchback for another 'example' like he's done to all his other victims?"

"Probably because the hunchback isn't one of the townfolk," Clint answered. "There haven't been any attempts on my life or the lives of O'Shea or any of his people."

"Any idea how we might try to catch the killer?" Connors said.

"We know he does his killing at night," the Gunsmith answered. "So that's when we'll have to watch for him."

"If this snow doesn't let up we probably won't even see the son of a bitch at night," Connors sighed.

"If this snow doesn't let up we might all be buried under it in a few more days anyway," Clint muttered. "But watching for the murderer to make his move after dark is the only way we're going to catch him at this rate."

"Maybe he'll stop now," Connors remarked, but his tone suggested he knew better.

"The killings won't stop until we stop the bastard for good," Clint told the lawman. "And we'd better do it soon or Ten Pines is going to be a town full of corpses."

TWENTY

Later that day the people of Ten Pines buried their dead. Joe Kirby, Edward Colby, and Father Flynn were lowered into three deep holes in the ground which had been painstakingly dug by shoveling through snow and ice and picking their way through frozen earth with axes, picks, and spades.

Mayor Colby spoke by the grave sites. He led the prayer that God would receive the departed souls of the three slain citizens. He prayed that justice would triumph and that the murderer of his son and the others would soon face the ultimate judgment of the Almighty.

The Gunsmith attended the funeral in order to observe mourners. Maybe the murderer's morbid curiosity or sense of guilt would lure the killer to the grave site.

Of course, there was no way of knowing if the murderer was present or not. Clint couldn't read minds, but he could watch for reactions on the faces of those assembled. Aside from the predictable sadness, Clint didn't see anything suspicious.

After the funeral, the Gunsmith checked on his horses and wagon in the livery stable. Assured that all was well with his horses and property, Clint stepped outside. The sky was dark. Snow continued to fall. The drifts seemed more like the walls of a white valley surrounding Ten Pines.

"Nightfall," Clint whispered aloud, voicing his thoughts to himself. "I wonder if he'll strike again tonight?"

The Gunsmith decided to combat the chill with a good stiff drink. He also wanted to talk to the bartender. Nobody hears more gossip or learns more about people's personalities than the local bartender.

Clint trudged through the knee-deep snow to the saloon, and entered. Harry was on duty behind the bar. A pair of middle-aged men sat at a table, playing poker for matchsticks. Clint had seen them at the funeral. He believed one man was the local cobbler, but he couldn't even guess what the other man did for a living. However, the third customer interested the Gunsmith the most.

He had never seen this man before. A tall stranger with a pot belly and broad shoulders, the man wore a dripping wet coat and a dark blue stetson. His profile resembled a bird of prey. A shaggy brown mustache decorated his upper lip beneath a hawk-billed nose.

As Clint approached the bar, the stranger turned. A black leather patch covered his right eye. The handle of a British-made Tranter revolver jutted from a belly holster on his belt.

"Howdy, Clint," Harry greeted. "You want a beer?"

"A shot of whiskey," Clint replied. "And I'll buy this fella a drink, too."

"Much obliged, friend," the one-eyed man said with a Virginian drawl. "I'll have a shot of red-eye, too."

"You're new in town, aren't you?" the Gunsmith asked, leaning an elbow on the counter.

"Bartender called you Clint," the stranger remarked. "My name's Sam Dobbs. I just kind'a wandered into Ten Pines. Darned lucky for me I did. Might'a froze to death in this weather."

Clint heard someone enter the saloon behind him. He glanced over his shoulder and discovered Thrasher and Crusher had come into the saloon. The two Chicago muscle boys glared at the Gunsmith.

"Clint," Harry the bartender began, "I reckon you might want'a talk to Sam here."

"I plan to," Clint said, not wishing to take his eyes off Thrasher and Crusher.

"Well, Sam is lookin' for that feller you seen the other day," Harry explained. "You know, the hunchback?"

Clint whirled to stare at the one-eyed man.

"You know about the hunchback?" he asked eagerly.

"Surely do," Sam Dobbs confirmed. "That's why I'm here in Ten Pines. Figure the bastard must've ducked into this town for shelter from the storm."

"Mister," the Gunsmith sighed with relief, "you have no idea how glad I am to meet you."

Without warning, two powerful arms seized Clint from behind. His assailant spun him around, pinning Clint's arms in a bear-hug hold. A fist crashed into the Gunsmith's jaw. Lights and pain exploded inside his head.

"We're gonna get some answers outta you now, Adams," Thrasher's voice bellowed.

The prizefighter rammed an uppercut to Clint's

stomach. The Gunsmith groaned and doubled up. Crusher altered his hold from a bear-hug to a half-nelson. His free hand plucked Clint's .45 Colt from his holster and dropped it to the floor.

"Hey, you fellers stop that right now," Harry began lamely.

"Keep outta this if you want to stay healthy," Thrasher warned.

He swung another fist to Clint's face. The Gunsmith fell back against Crusher. The wrestler snaked his arm under Clint's right arm to clasp both hands at the back of the Gunsmith's neck. Thrasher punched Clint in the stomach again.

"I'm gonna smash your guts in if you don't talk, damn it." Thrasher snarled as he reared back his fist.

The Gunsmith bent a knee and quickly raised it. Thrasher's fist collided with Clint's kneecap. The boxer grunted when he bruised a knuckle on the hard surface.

Clint suddenly thrust both feet into Thrasher's chest. The kick sent him staggering backward. The Gunsmith braced both his hands against his forehead to reduce the pressure of the wrestler's half-nelson hold. Then he stomped his boot heel on Crusher's instep.

The wrestler bellowed with rage. He quickly pivoted, pushing a hip against the Gunsmith's buttocks. The big man kept an arm hooked under Clint's right armpit and pulled hard. The Gunsmith hurled over Crusher's hip and crashed to the floor hard.

Clint tried to scramble upright. Crusher swung his big boot to the Gunsmith's ribs and kicked him across the floor into the wooden legs of a table and chairs. Clint was vaguely aware of shouts and curses from Harry and the two poker players. Christ, he thought.

What's their problem? I'm the one who's getting beat up.

Crusher stomped forward and launched another kick at the Gunsmith. Clint slithered under the table to avoid the wrestler's boot. The Gunsmith quickly rose up beneath the table, sending the furniture hurtling into Crusher. The wrestler stumbled back against the bar, but Thrasher moved in like a charging bull.

A left jab hit Clint in the breastbone. Thrasher jabbed again, his first tagging Clint on the chin. The Gunsmith's head bounced back violently from the punch. The prizefighter followed up with a right cross.

Clint dodged the attack. Thrasher's body pivoted off balance, thrown forward by his own momentum. The Gunsmith hooked a sly left to the pugilist's kidney and drove a right uppercut under the big man's ribs. Thrasher didn't even grunt. He whirled and lashed a backfist at Clint's face.

The Gunsmith was propelled right into Crusher. The wrestler grabbed Clint's shirt front in one hand and clawed the other into the Gunsmith's crotch. Crusher abruptly picked up Clint and hurled him over the top of the bar. The Gunsmith crashed down behind the bar. His head swam along the brink of unconsciousness, and his body felt as if he'd been caught in a stampede. Clint was tempted to just lie there and pass out peacefully, but he realized Thrasher and Crusher would not grant him that luxury.

The harsh report of a pistol shot startled Clint into his full senses. Could it be somebody had fired the shot to stop the fight? He hoped that meant somebody had put a bullet in either Thrasher or Crusher.

"That's enough," Sam Dobbs' voice ordered.

Clint Adams slowly rose to his feet, leaning against

the bar to keep his balance as his head began to clear. Dobbs held his Tranter revolver aimed at Thrasher and Crusher. The two muscle-bound hoodlums held their hands overhead. The Gunsmith sighed with relief.

"This ain't none of your business, Mr. One-Eye," Crusher snapped.

"Don't seem like a very fair fight to me," Dobbs commented, "two against one. You fellas want to fight him? Do it one at a time."

"Sam," Clint said tensely, "take a look at those monsters. Either one of them is as big as two regular men."

"What do you want me to do?" Dobbs shrugged. "Shrink 'em?"

"You have a seat, Thrash," Crusher told his partner. "I'll take care of Adams."

The wrestler rubbed his hands together and grinned as he approached the bar. Clint turned sharply and reached for the bottles of red-eye on the shelf behind the bar. He grabbed two bottles and threw them at Crusher as fast as he could.

One projectile missed, and glass shattered against the floor, splashing whiskey in all directions. The other bottle bounced off the wrestler's thick shoulder and shattered against a tabletop.

Crusher kept coming, an angry snarl plastered on his ugly face. The Gunsmith only had one thing left to throw at the wrestler. Clint grabbed the countertop with both hands and swung his legs over the bar. He hurtled forward, feet first.

Clint's boots slammed into Crusher's chest. The wrestler staggered from the unexpected blow. Clint immediately clasped both hands together and swung them at Crusher's jaw. The wrestler's head barely moved from a blow which would have rendered most men unconscious. Clint didn't waste time admiring his opponent's endurance.

The Gunsmith hooked a left to the side of Crusher's skull. It felt as if he'd tried to punch out a marble statue. Clint swung an uppercut under the wrestler's jaw. Crusher suddenly grabbed Clint's arm and swung him around like a hammer-thrower.

Crusher released Clint. The Gunsmith flew across the room and crashed into a set of chairs and a table. Man and furniture toppled to the floor. The wrestler charged forward, determined to finish off the Gunsmith.

Clint bolted from the floor and scooped up a chair. He lunged forward and thrust the ends of two chair legs into the wrestler's lower body. Crusher uttered a choking gasp and doubled up.

The Gunsmith raised the chair and swung it with all his might. The chair shattered on impact against Crusher's head and shoulders. The wrestler fell face first to the floor. Clint raised a boot and ruthlessly stomped the heel behind Crusher's ear to make certain the big man wouldn't get up again.

"Son of a bitch," Thrasher growled as he shuffled forward, fists poised.

"Wait a minute," Clint snapped breathlessly. "Don't I get a minute or two to rest before I have to fight this ape?"

"Seems fair to me," Dobbs declared.

"How about a beer, Harry?" Clint asked. "I'll even buy one for Thrasher."

"Who the hell is going to pay for all this damage?" Harry replied, gazing about at the shambles which had been his saloon.

"Let's figure that out later," the Gunsmith urged.

"Shit," Thrasher growled. "Pour the goddamn beer so Adams can drink some courage and let's get on with the fight."

The Gunsmith and Thrasher moved toward the bar. Dobbs still stood with his revolver in hand. Harry shook his head with dismay as he poured two beers. Crusher lay unconscious, not uttering a sound.

"What the hell is going on in here?" Sheriff Connors demanded, marching through the entrance of the saloon.

"It'll only take a minute," Thrasher said, turning to face the lawman.

He also turned his back on the Gunsmith. Clint immediately took advantage of this opportunity. He stepped forward and lashed out a kick. The toe of his boot landed between the boxer's legs, smashing Thrasher's testicles. The pugilist shrieked in agony.

"Jesus," Connors gasped.

Clint pounced on Thrasher's back, snaking an arm around the larger man's neck. His forearm closed off Thrasher's throat. His fist struck the pugilist in a kidney. Clint pulled Thrasher backward and rammed a knee into the small of his spine.

"My God, Adams!" the sheriff shouted. "Stop that. You're gonna kill him!"

"Somebody has to," the Gunsmith replied through clenched teeth as he continued to throttle his opponent.

Thrasher struggled violently. He drove an elbow back into Clint's ribs. The Gunsmith groaned and quickly hammered his fist into the boxer's temple. Thrasher moaned, but tried another elbow stroke. Clint didn't want a broken rib driven into a lung. He released Thrasher.

The pugilist whirled and delivered a quick jab to Clint's chin. The blow stung, but it lacked his usual force. The larger man had been weakened by Clint's combination of choking and battering.

Clint danced out of range of another jab and swung a left hook at Thrasher's face. The boxer blocked with a right forearm and tried his own left. The Gunsmith deflected the punch with an elbow and promptly kicked Thrasher in the crotch again.

This time the pugilist uttered an ugly gurgle, his mouth open in a small black oval of mute agony. He clasped both hands to his battered genitals and began to sink to his knees. The Gunsmith hit him one more time, throwing all his weight behind a powerful right cross.

Thrasher fell to the floor hard. He sprawled on his belly in a senseless lump. Clint stepped back, rubbing his bruised and bleeding knuckles.

"Mighty fine fightin', Clint," Sam Dobbs declared as he handed the Gunsmith his modified Colt revolver. "That was some of the best dirty fightin' I've seen since the War Between the States."

"Adams, I ought'a arrest you for disturbin' the peace, destruction of private property, and whatever else I can come up with," Connors said angrily.

"Sheriff," the Gunsmith replied, panting hard as he struggled to catch his breath. "Shut up."

TWENTY-ONE

"What do you mean by tellin' me to shut up?" the sheriff demanded.

"Shut up means close your mouth and listen," the Gunsmith explained. "Mr. Dobbs here has something to tell you."

"My name is Sam Dobbs, Sheriff," the one-eyed stranger declared as he held open his coat to reveal a copper badge pinned to his shirt. "I'm a United States federal marshal."

"Pleased to meet you, Dobbs," Connors said gruffly. "But what the hell are you doing in Ten Pines?"

"Lookin' for a killer," Dobbs explained. "A fella named John Bates. Not likely you could mistake him for anybody else. Bates is a hunchback with a shaggy black beard."

"Do tell?" Connors raised his eyebrows. "I reckon I owe you an apology, Clint."

"Forget it," the Gunsmith assured him. He noticed, however, that the sheriff had called him by his first name. "Sam, tell us about this killer."

"Bates is plum loco," Dobbs began. "He's got some sort of crazy notion about certain positions of the stars being signals that he ought'a kill somebody.

131

Bates is a drunkard. Probably sees these 'visions' when he passes out."

"And during these 'visions' Bates gets messages to go kill people?" Clint frowned. "Look, Sam, we've had three nasty murders and none of them were committed by a drunk having delusions."

"Apparently Bates doesn't get violent when he's drunk," Dobbs explained. "But he remembers his crazy dreams and figures it's a divine message or somethin'. He's usually cold sober when he does the killin'. Turns it into a goddamn ritual."

"That explains a lot," Connors stated. "But how do you know so much about this hunchback?"

"Because I tracked him down and arrested the bastard," Dobbs explained. "Had him prisoner and planned to take him to trial. Hauled Bates through the forest for two days and nights. Chained him to a tree before I'd close my eyes. Checked him for weapons every morning. I still don't know how he managed to free himself."

"You're lucky he didn't cut your throat," Connors remarked.

"I woke up before he had a chance to get to my gear," Dobbs explained. "Took a shot at him, but the weather was my biggest problem. Couldn't see a clear target through all that snow. Bates melted into the forest and I've been trackin' him ever since. No small chore. This damn snow has covered the bastard's tracks. Still, Ten Pines seemed to be the most logical place for him to run to."

"I reckon this is where he wound up," Connors agreed.

"What kind of weapons does Bates favor, Dobbs?" the Gunsmith asked.

"Uses a knife mostly," Dobbs answered. "But he's been known to use a gun from time to time, and he's also used other sorts of weapons. One time he strangled a feller to death with a strand of barbed wire. Another time he smashed in a minister's skull with a candlestick from the altar. Murdered the preacher right in his own church, if you can believe it."

"We can believe it all right," Connors assured him. "The son of a bitch has a new trick. He drove a spike through the forehead of our priest."

"God Almighty," Dobbs gasped. "Feel kind'a like this is my fault. If I'd followed my instincts and killed Bates as soon as I found him, none of this would have happened to you folks."

"Well, we'll take care of that problem now," Sheriff Connors declared. "I'm gonna get everybody in town together and tell them to shoot that hunchback bastard on sight."

"Wait a minute, Sheriff," Clint began. "Let's—"

A sudden movement caught his attention. Clint glimpsed the motion via the corner of an eye. He whirled toward it, hand streaking to the modified Colt on his hip. Thrasher had risen to his knees, a Police Colt in his fist. The pugilist's blood-streaked face was a mask of fury as he cocked the hammer of his pistol.

The Gunsmith's revolver cleared leather and roared before Thrasher could squeeze the trigger of his gun. The pugilist's face exploded like a miniature volcano, splattering blood and brains against the framework of the bar.

Sam Dobbs abruptly shoved the Gunsmith, sending Clint staggering into a wall. The Gunsmith managed to restrain the automatic impulse to open fire on the marshal when he saw the Tranter in Dobbs' hand. But

Dobbs didn't aim his weapon at Clint.

The Tranter boomed. Crusher cried out as a .45-caliber slug slammed into his broad chest. The wrestler held his Police Colt in his fist, thumb poised on the hammer. Dobbs fired his pistol again. The second bullet drilled Crusher right through the heart. The brute flopped on the floor like a beached whale, his muscles relaxing as the last trace of life vanished.

"You all right, Clint?" Dobbs asked, holstering his Tranter.

"Yeah," the Gunsmith replied as he returned his Colt to leather. "Thanks to you, Sam."

"You'd have done the same for me, I reckon," the marshal stated. "Who were these two fellas anyway?"

"A couple polecats who worked for a jasper who I've gotta have a talk with," Clint declared.

The Gunsmith headed for the door. Sheriff Connors followed right behind him. The lawman grabbed Clint's sheepskin jacket, but the Gunsmith thrust a forearm against Connors' wrist to break his grip.

"Hands off, fella," Clint warned, his eyes slits of controlled rage, colder than the icy wind outside.

"Then tell me what you intend to do to Richard O'Shea?" the sheriff demanded.

"That'll depend on him," the Gunsmith replied simply.

TWENTY-TWO

Clint Adams waded through the formidable sea of snow, heading for the hotel. Sheriff Connors followed the Gunsmith, cursing as he tried to catch up with Clint. The Gunsmith's long stride and determined step gave him a good head start, and he kept several yards in front of the lawman as he reached his destination.

Clint opened the door and entered the lobby, hand poised by the butt of his .45 Colt. The lobby was deserted. Clint moved to the front desk and checked behind it to be certain no one was hidden there. The Gunsmith headed for the stairs.

Frank Cameron stood at the head of the stairs, calmly waiting for Clint Adams. The gunfighter hooked his thumbs in his gunbelt near the buckle, offering no immediate threat. Yet, he stood with his feet spread shoulder-width apart. Cameron clearly had no intention of moving.

"Good evenin', Clint," the gunman greeted with a formal nod.

"Hello, Frank," the Gunsmith replied as he moved to the foot of the stairs. "Something on your mind?"

"Reckon so," Cameron admitted, nodding in reply.

Sheriff Connors entered the lobby. He saw Clint at the bottom of the stairs, gazing up at Frank Cameron.

The Gunsmith unbuttoned his sheepskin jacket to allow fast access to his modified Colt. Cameron slowly moved his hands, shifting the right toward the Smith & Wesson.

"Hold on, you two," Connors snapped. "There's been enough killin' in this town."

"Keep out of this, Sheriff," Clint warned. "Frank, I've got to speak to Richard O'Shea. Why don't you just step aside?"

"You know why, Clint," Cameron answered. "I can't let you up these stairs."

"Then tell O'Shea I want to talk to him," Clint urged. "Just talk. I won't gun him down in cold blood."

"He told me to stop you, Clint," the gunfighter sighed. "O'Shea ain't comin' out, and you ain't comin' up here."

"I don't want to kill you, Frank," the Gunsmith told him.

"I ain't got no grudge against you neither," Cameron answered. "But I'm bein' paid to do a job. Right now, that job is to kill you."

"Now, hold on!" Connors shouted. "This has gone far enough!"

"You'd better stand clear of the line of fire, Sheriff," the Gunsmith warned. "Frank, is there any other way we can settle this?"

"Yeah," Cameron answered. "You can get in your wagon, with that fancy black Arabian hitched to the rear of the rig and ride outta town."

"I can't do that," Clint stated. "Not in the middle of a snow blizzard."

"I know," the gunfighter nodded. "So I reckon there ain't no other way."

"I reckon not," the Gunsmith sighed.

"Ain't personal, Clint," Cameron assured him. "Just business."

"Yeah," Clint replied simply. "Make your move, friend."

"I'd be obliged if you—" Cameron began.

The gunfighter suddenly reached for his pistol, hoping to catch Clint off guard. The Gunsmith's Colt cleared leather. Connors hadn't even seen Clint's arm move, but the gun was in his fist. Clint Adams fired two rounds. Yellow flame spat from the muzzle of his pistol, jutting up the staircase like the tongue of a dragon.

Frank Cameron stumbled from side to side like a drunkard. His fist clenched the grip of his Smith & Wesson, the barrel caught on the edge of his holster. Cameron coughed, and blood spewed from his lips. The pistol tumbled from his grasp and landed on the floor boards by his feet.

"Mighty fast, Adams . . ." the gunfighter croaked.

Cameron fell forward. He plunged down the stairs, rolling against the risers clumsily. The Gunsmith stepped aside and allowed Cameron's body to tumble past him. The gunfighter's lifeless form sprawled out at the foot of the stairs.

"Jesus," Sheriff Connors rasped.

The Gunsmith glanced down at Frank Cameron's body. The gunfighter had been shot twice through the heart. Clint shook his head sadly. Cameron had forced his hand. Clint found no pleasure in killing.

Clint Adams stepped over the dead man and mounted the stairs. Sheriff Connors shouted something at the Gunsmith, but Clint ignored him and continued to climb up the steps. He held the modified Colt in his fist, smoke still drifting from its hot muzzle.

"O'Shea!" the Gunsmith shouted. "Come on out. There's nobody left now but you and me. We can either talk or you can try to shoot it out with me, fat man!"

He reached the head of the stairs. Clint noticed the door to O'Shea's room was open. He glanced down both ends of the corridor, looking for the Chicago hoodlum. Richard O'Shea seemed to have vanished.

Suddenly an arm appeared around the doorway to the Irishman's room. Clint crouched low. He saw a .32 Smith & Wesson short-barreled revolver in a pudgy hand. The pocket pistol barked and a tiny slug splintered wood from the balustrade post near Clint's head.

The Gunsmith swung his pistol toward the door and got off two rounds. Richard O'Shea screamed when one bullet split O'Shea's forearm, breaking the bone, and the other slug shattered O'Shea's elbow.

The .32 pistol fell from his useless fingers. O'Shea fell across the threshold and landed in the hallway, clutching his bullet-crushed arm. The Gunsmith didn't drop his guard as he approached the wounded hoodlum. An injured man can be more dangerous than a whole one if he's desperate enough.

Clint kicked the diminutive Smith & Wesson out of O'Shea's reach. The Irishman glared up at him. Hatred and fear combined with pain to create a hideous expression which barely seemed human.

"You lose, O'Shea," Clint told him, aiming his Colt at the Irishman's face.

"Goddamn you!" O'Shea hissed through clenched teeth. "Goddamn you and those dago bastards."

"Adams!" Sheriff Connors snapped as he galloped

up the stairs behind the Gunsmith. "What in blue-blazin' hell is goin' on?"

"Ask O'Shea," Clint replied calmly. "He's the one who started the trouble in the first place."

"You mean O'Shea was involved in the murders?" Connors shook his head. "But we just found out the hunchback done that."

"No," the Gunsmith replied. "I don't mean the murders, Sheriff. O'Shea wasn't responsible for any of them, but he figured *I was*. This idiot figured I dynamited the hotel in an attempt to kill him. Ain't that right, O'Shea?"

"I know you done it, Adams," the Irishman groaned, cradling his shattered limb with his other arm. "Why else would anybody have blown up the hotel except to try to kill me? The goddamn dagos hired you to murder me."

"You think I'd set off the dynamite in the wrong room?" Clint asked. "Figure I'm that stupid?"

"Probably planned to lure me outside and kill me," O'Shea answered. "That's why I didn't leave my room. Haven't left it all day, until now."

"You horse's ass," Connors snorted. "Didn't you know Joe Kirby had been knifed to death before that explosion occurred?"

"Kirby probably caught Adams tryin' to sneak the dynamite outta his wagon," O'Shea explained. "He had to kill the poor bastard to keep everybody from knowin' he dynamited the hotel."

"I could have killed you the first time we met, O'Shea," Clint remarked. "Why do you figure I spared you then?"

"The desk clerk was a witness," O'Shea answered. "So you figured there'd be a better chance later."

"This feller's loco," Connors sighed.

"O'Shea has been obsessed with the idea Italian criminals have been tracking him ever since he left Chicago," Clint explained. "His own fears have created enemies which never existed. That's why he figured I wanted to kill him."

"So he sent his two muscle boys after you?" Connors mused. "They were supposed to beat a confession outta you. Then he told Cameron to take care of you when he saw you headin' for the hotel."

"That's about the size of it," the Gunsmith nodded. "This terrified idiot got three men killed for nothing."

"Didn't he wonder about Father Flynn?" Connors asked. "How would the murder of a priest fit in with his notions?"

"I don't think O'Shea knew about Flynn," Clint answered. "You heard him. He's been hiding in his room all day. None of his people attended the funeral either, so I reckon he didn't have any idea the priest had been killed. Even if he did, I'm sure he would have come up with some sort of crazy explanation to blame me for it."

"How about it, O'Shea?" Connors inquired. "Are you really that loco?"

O'Shea didn't answer. He was too busy trying to reach under his jacket for an object which formed a small lump at the small of his spine. The Gunsmith quickly stomped on O'Shea's bullet-smashed arm. The Irishman shrieked and promptly fainted.

"Damn, Adams," the sheriff muttered. "That was an awful mean thing to do."

"Not really," Clint replied mildly as he knelt beside O'Shea. "Just had to disarm him."

The Gunsmith peeled back O'Shea's coattails to

reveal a Remington derringer tucked into the waist band of his trousers at the small of his back. Clint took the tiny pistol and slipped it into the pocket of his sheepskin jacket.

TWENTY-THREE

Sandra opened her door and cautiously peered into the hallway. She poked her pretty blonde head outside and cleared her throat to get the attention of Clint Adams and Sheriff Connors.

"Excuse me," Sandra called softly. "But have you gents finished shootin' at each other for a while?"

"It's over for now," Clint replied. "Sorry, Sandra. Your boy friend Richard got himself in a heap of trouble tonight."

"Looks like it," she said, gazing down at O'Shea. "Is he dead, Clint?"

"No," the Gunsmith told her. "But Thrasher, Crusher, and Frank Cameron are."

"Wondered why there was so much shootin' going on," the woman commented. "Well, I never liked those fellas much anyway."

"I hope you aren't going to miss O'Shea too much either," the Gunsmith remarked. "Sheriff, will you help me get this man down the stairs?"

"What for?" Connors asked, puzzled by the request.

"I thought we might take him over to your jail and lock him in a nice, cozy cell where he can't cause any more trouble."

"Oh," the sheriff nodded, embarrassed that he

hadn't suggested the idea first. "Don't reckon it'd be a good idea to just leave him runnin' around free."

"I think I'd be a bit uncomfortable if I knew he was still loose," the Gunsmith confessed. "Besides, he's going to need medical care, or he'll lose that arm for sure."

"My God," Sandra gasped when she saw the bloodied, mangled condition of O'Shea's limb. "Richard and me haven't been very close for some time, but I never wanted anything like this to happen to him."

"He dealt the cards," Clint told her. "I just had to play the game the way he chose—and he lost."

"Uh, Adams," Connors began. "You want'a do anything with her?"

The Gunsmith raised his eyebrows. Sandra grinned.

"I mean," the sheriff said awkwardly, "she's sort of a member of O'Shea's gang, ain't she?"

"Relax, Sheriff," Sandra urged, an amused smile on her face. "I don't plan to hurt anybody. Trust me."

"Well," the sheriff began, "I reckon that'll be all right."

"Let's take care of O'Shea," Clint urged. "Then we can concentrate on finding our killer."

The Gunsmith and Connors half-dragged, half-carried O'Shea down the stairs. Blood dripped from the bullet wounds in the Irishman's shattered arm. A crowd had formed in front of the hotel. Harry the bartender and Sherman Colby waited in the lobby. Harry carried his double-barreled Greener, and Sherman had a .45 Colt revolver.

"Need any help, Sheriff?" Harry inquired when he saw the two men haul O'Shea down the stairs.

"Thanks," Connors replied. "This feller ain't skinny."

Harry assisted Clint and the sheriff with O'Shea. Sherman Colby holstered his weapon and hurried from the hotel, apparently afraid he too might be put to work. The rest of the crowd moved away as O'Shea was transported outside.

The icy wind hit the Gunsmith, Connors, and Harry like a burst of frozen buckshot pellets. Sherman Colby jogged through the snow in a leaping gait, eager to return to his restaurant. Clint caught a glimpse of Lilly's face at the window of the eatery. She smiled at him as the Gunsmith and his allies dragged O'Shea toard the jail.

"What . . ." the Irishman groaned as the cold wind abruptly pulled him back to consciousness. "What the hell is goin' on?"

"Relax, feller," Connors told him. "It'll be nice and warm in my jail."

"Harry," Clint began, "I think we can handle O'Shea the rest of the way. Why don't you go fetch the doctor?"

"Sure enough," the bartender agreed.

Harry plunged through the deep snow toward the doctor's office while Clint and Connors continued to haul the shivering Irishman to the jail.

Suddenly, a violent explosion blasted the sky with a glare of orange hell fire. The Gunsmith and the sheriff hit the ground, dragging O'Shea with them. Snow poured over their necks and slid down the backs of their collars. O'Shea cried out in terror. The Gunsmith rolled onto his back and yanked his pistol from its holster.

The restaurant was gone. Instead of the building, a pile of smoking rubble sprawled across the plankwalk into the street. Debris still hurtled through the sky as the Gunsmith rose up from the snow.

"Lilly!" he exclaimed, running toward the wreckage.

Another, smaller explosion erupted and more debris leapt into the air. Clint threw himself to the ground once more, managing to keep his revolver clear of the snow. Something fell beside Clint. He heard the angry sizzle of a chunk of burning wood as it sunk into a drift.

The Gunsmith scrambled upright again and bolted for the shelter of a cobbler's shop. Clint approached the mangled remnants of the restaurant. A bloody leg, severed at the knee, jutted from a pile of broken boards and shattered furniture. The limb had been a man's, a low-heeled boot still on the foot. Clint saw the pulverized corpse of Sherman Colby amid another pile of rubble.

Clint moved past the man's body and searched among the burning ruins. He found what he was looking for—yet hoped wouldn't be there. Lilly lay under a lump of wreckage. A splintered table leg was buried in her chest. The wooden shaft protruded between Lilly's beautiful breasts. Her lifeless, unseeing eyes stared up at the night sky.

"Oh shit," Clint hissed in helpless rage as he gazed down at the horrible corpse of a woman he had liked as a person and a lover.

The Gunsmith scanned the surrounding buildings, praying that God would grant him one favor. Just give me a clear shot at the son of a bitch who killed Lilly, he thought. Give me a chance to put a bullet in his rotten guts.

But he didn't get a clear target. A number of frightened citizens ventured from homes and businesses. They stood on the plankwalks, horrified expressions plastered on their pale faces. The Gunsmith didn't see John Bates, the hunchback fugitive Marshal Sam Dobbs claimed was a killer.

As a matter of fact, Clint didn't see Dobbs either.

The Gunsmith holstered his Colt revolver and turned his attention to the sheriff's office. Richard O'Shea crawled to the plankwalk, still nursing his damaged arm. Sheriff Connors, however, lay spread eagle in the snow. The Gunsmith jogged to the fallen lawman.

"Hey, Sheriff," Clint began, reaching down to help Connors, "were you hit by something from the explosion?"

Then Clint noticed the crimson hole in the side of the sheriff's head. Part of his skull was missing. Blood and brains were spilled across the snow beside Connor's corpse.

"Christ, what a night," the Gunsmith rasped.

TWENTY-FOUR

Harry the bartender returned. When he saw the motionless figure of Sheriff Connors in the snow, Harry came to such an abrupt halt, he lost his balance and fell to all fours. The Gunsmith helped him to his feet.

"I . . . I heard the explosion, but I kept goin'," Harry explained, spitting out a mouthful of snow. "I couldn't find Doc Kirby in his office so I went around back to his house. He was inside. Passed out next to an empty bottle of red-eye."

"Shit," Clint growled. "That's just great."

"What are we gonna do, Clint?" the bartender asked. "The sheriff is hurt too."

"Sheriff doesn't need a doctor," the Gunsmith explained. "He's already dead."

"Jesus, Mary, and Joseph!" Harry gasped.

"Sherman Colby and Lilly are dead, too," Clint added. "Goddamn explosion killed 'em both."

"Is that what happened to the sheriff?" Harry asked.

"I don't think so," the Gunsmith replied. "Looks like somebody put a bullet through the side of his head. Probably shot him when the second explosion went

149

off. Wouldn't surprise me if the killer set the second blast to go off to serve as cover for the report of his gunshot. Clever bastard.''

"My God, Clint," Harry whispered. "This was just a quiet little town where nothin' ever happened. What in hell is goin' on?"

"A lot of people are getting killed," the Gunsmith said dryly. "Help me get O'Shea into the jail."

"You aren't gonna just lock him in a cell are you?" Harry asked.

"I'm not gonna leave him out here to freeze to death," Clint answered. "Come on."

They dragged the wounded Irishman into the sheriff's office. The Gunsmith found the keys to the cells and unlocked one of the cages. Harry helped Clint haul O'Shea into the cell. They lowered him onto a cot.

"Christ, I hurt," the Chicago-bred hoodlum groaned. "You gonna get the doctor for me, Adams?"

"Don't worry about a thing, fella," the Gunsmith replied. "It won't help a damn thing."

Without warning, Clint punched O'Shea on the point of his chin. The Irishman's eyes rolled up into his head and he slumped unconscious.

"What you do that for?" Harry asked, startled by the Gunsmith's actions.

"Because he's better off if he isn't awake when we start cutting those bullets out of his arm," Clint answered.

"*We?*" the bartender stared at him.

"See if you can find a bottle of whiskey in Connors' office," the Gunsmith instructed as he took a stockman's knife from his pocket and snapped open the blade.

"Good idea," Harry said. "I could sure use a drink."

"You can have one later," Clint told him. "We need steady hands and calm heads right now. We'll also need some clean cloth and something to make a splint with. A couple sticks or something like that."

"I'll find that stuff," Harry agreed. "But you'll do the cutting, right?"

"Yeah," the Gunsmith agreed as he took some matches from an oilcloth wrapper and made certain they were dry. "I'll do the cutting."

Harry found everything Clint needed. The Gunsmith brought a coal oil lamp into the cell, removed the globe and lit the wick. He turned up the flame and used it to sterilize the blade of his knife.

"Now hold the lamp over here so I can see what I'm doing," Clint told Harry.

"All right," the bartender agreed, watching the Gunsmith pour some whiskey along the knife blade. "Can't I just have one swallow of that red-eye now?"

"O'Shea is apt to need it more than either of us," Clint explained. "When he comes around, he'll be doing a lot of hurting. He'll also need to have that damn doctor. And he'll need him *sober*."

"That's not so easy with Doc Kirby," Harry remarked. "Feller is drunk most of the time."

"Worry about that later," Clint said as he washed some whiskey over his hands. "We got a job to do now."

Clint had already torn open the sleeve to O'Shea's right arm and washed some whiskey over the wounds. One bullet had passed clean through the Irishman's forearm, but the other was lodged in what remained of

O'Shea's elbow. Clint clenched his teeth and inserted the tip of the blade. He probed inside the wound, prying out several small chunks of bone and cartilage. Blood gushed from the hole, despite the tourniquet tied to the injured arm.

Clint's stomach knotted and convulsed as he poked and scraped inside the wound. O'Shea suddenly screamed and almost bolted upright. The Gunsmith and Harry pinned him to the cot. The Irishman uttered a faint whimper and passed out again.

At last, Clint fished out a small glob of lead. He tossed the bullet aside and bandaged the gaping wound. Harry sighed with relief.

"Thank God that's over," the bartender whispered.

"Don't thank Him yet," the Gunsmith warned. "O'Shea's elbow joint has been pulverized. There's no sense in putting a splint on his arm.

"What do you mean?" Harry asked, certain he didn't want to hear the reply.

"I mean we're going to have to amputate," Clint replied grimly.

"Like hell," the bartender rasped. "I ain't gonna help you cut a man's arm off, Clint."

"Then you can be the one to put a bullet through his brain, Harry," the Gunsmith said sharply. "If we don't amputate, the poison will spread through his body. Gangrene is an ugly way to die. You want to sign this fella's death warrant? Then you execute him."

"Hell, Clint," Harry groaned. "I'm about ready to throw up as it is."

"Me, too," the Gunsmith confessed. "But we still have to do it."

''All right,'' Harry agreed reluctantly. ''How do we do this?''

''Well,'' the Gunsmith sighed. ''I'm going to need a bone saw. . . .''

TWENTY-FIVE

Marshal Sam Dobbs arrived at the jail as the Gunsmith and Harry were about to amputate Richard O'Shea's arm. The one-eyed lawman glanced down at the tray of instruments, catgut, and ether bottle on a chair beside the cot.

"You boys know what you're doin' here?" Dobbs inquired.

"We're trying," the Gunsmith replied. "I don't suppose you're familiar with cutting off arms by any chance."

"As a matter of fact," the marshal began, "I helped amputate a few limbs off injured soldiers during the War."

"Then you're elected," the Gunsmith replied with relief.

"Where'd you get the instruments from?" Dobbs asked, rolling up his sleeves.

"Got 'em from the doctor's office," Harry answered.

"How come you didn't bring the doctor as well?" the marshal asked. "Don't tell me he's dead, too."

"Dead drunk," Clint explained. "Are you willing to do the cutting, Sam?"

"Reckon I'd better," Dobbs answered. "Put some cloth over this man's nose and mouth. Then put three drops of ether on the cloth. No more than that. You can kill a man with that stuff if you're not careful. And don't light any matches near the ether.''

"I know," Clint nodded.

"What happened to this fella?" Dobbs asked as he took up the bone saw. "Hurt in the explosion?"

"I shot him," the Gunsmith replied.

They spoke very little as the marshal supervised the grim task of amputating O'Shea's arm. Dobbs sawed through the limb at the elbow and cut it off in less than a minute. Harry grabbed his mouth and bolted from the cell. Clint heard the bartender vomit as Dobbs inspected the bloody stump of O'Shea's arm.

"Looks pretty clean here," the marshal commented, probing the gory limb with a scapel. "I take it you already done some work on him."

"I took the bullet out," Clint replied, wishing he could follow Harry's example.

"Good work," Dobbs told him. "Well, let's cauterize the stump and sew him up."

The experience was one of the most awful, stomach-churning ordeals Clint had ever participated in. Every sense was subjected to horror. The sight of Dobbs cutting and whittling away on the stump. The stench of burnt flesh as the wound was cauterized. The sound of O'Shea's moans everytime he neared the brink of consciousness.

The Gunsmith admired Dobbs' nerve. The marshal grimly carried out the grisly chore with professional calm. Finally it was over. Dobbs put over a hundred stitches in the stump and wrapped it carefully with an improvised bandage.

"Well," the marshal sighed. "If shock doesn't kill him between now and sunup, he ought'a live.''

"I'm sure glad you were here, Sam," Clint stated. "Don't know if I could have done what you did."

"I think you would have, Clint," Dobbs assured him. "You and I are probably a lot alike. We try to do whatever circumstances require of us."

"Circumstances require we find that goddamn murderer," Clint said grimly. "Son of a bitch killed three more people tonight."

"Three?" Dobbs' single eyebrow rose.

"Yeah," the Gunsmith said. "Sheriff Connors, Sherman Colby who ran the restaurant, and a young woman named Lilly who worked there as a waitress."

"Oh, God," Dobbs shook his head sadly. "Well, I reckon Bates went on a rampage tonight."

"And it seems like he's pretty selective about his targets," Clint commented dryly.

"You think he wanted to kill an innocent young woman?" Dobbs asked. "What would his motive be? What reason would he have to kill anybody in Ten Pines?"

"I don't know," Clint admitted. "I don't know what reason anyone would have to murder any of the people who have been killed in this town."

"There you go, Clint," Dobbs announced. "These murders aren't committed by a man with reason. Bates is insane. We'll just have to concentrate on stopping the bastard and the hell with why he's doin' it."

"Maybe you're right, Sam," Clint said skeptically. The two men moved from the cell block. The Gunsmith closed the door to O'Shea's cage and locked it.

"That fella is gonna be mighty upset when he wakes up and finds his arm is gone," Dobbs stated. "Somebody ought'a stay here with him."

"I can move my gear in here," Clint shrugged.

"Maybe I ought to do it instead," Dobbs suggested. "After all, you shot the fella. He'll probably be more willin' to believe that arm had to come off if somebody else tells him."

"You may be right," the Gunsmith began. "By the way, where were you when the explosion occurred? I looked around for you and I didn't see you among the crowd."

"Oh, I moved behind some buildings to the north. Hoped I'd catch Bates, but I reckon he didn't head that way."

"Reckon not," Clint frowned. "You look familiar, Sam. Have we met before?"

"Not exactly," Dobbs smiled. "We sort of crossed paths once before."

"I think I remember now," Clint said. "It was in Windego City, right? I fixed a lot of guns that day. Was one of them your pistol?"

"That's right," the marshal confirmed. "This old Tranter had a busted firing pin."

"Windego is sure a wild town," Clint mused. "I left a couple days before that big fire burned down the Red Horse Saloon. Did you happen to see it?"

"I left before it happened too," Dobbs shrugged. "Heard it was one hell of a mess."

"Not as big a mess as the one we have here in Ten Pines," Clint remarked.

"That's a fact," the marshal agreed.

TWENTY-SIX

The Gunsmith left Dobbs at the sheriff's office. He noticed Harry loping through the snow drifts, heading back to his saloon. Clint turned up his collar to guard against the cold as he trudged through the downy white piles. Yet, he paid little attention to the weather. He didn't even notice that it was no longer snowing.

Clint glanced at the shattered wreckage which had formerly been the restaurant. Anger and grief boiled inside him. The bodies of Lilly and Sherman Colby were gone. Clint guessed the corpses had been taken to the church until they could receive a proper funeral.

The Gunsmith finally reached his destination. He moved to the rear of the building. The back door wasn't locked. Clint knocked, although he didn't expect the occupant to answer. Then he entered, pistol ready in his fist.

Clint had never been inside Doc Kirby's house before. He moved slowly through the shadows, every sense alert to possible danger. The foul odors of mildew, stale air, old urine, and fresh vomit nearly forced the Gunsmith to gag. Clutter was everywhere, and he tested each step with a probing toe before putting his foot down. Old newspapers and unwashed plates littered the floor.

The only light came from the edge of a half-open

door. Clint approached cautiously. He eased the door open with the fingertips of his left hand while the right held his .45 revolver ready for action.

A loud rasping, spitting noise erupted from the room within. Illuminated by a kerosene lamp on a dusty table, the room was a shambles. Cobwebs filled each corner. A poorly patched, old couch bled stuffing from its broken stitches, and several empty bottles lay beside it. A pile of leatherbound books had been heaped in the middle of the room.

Kneeling at the end of the couch, a lone figure bent his back as he held his face over the rim of a tin waste can. The man's hand grasped the sill of a window, pinning down fabric of filthy gray curtains. He vomited into the can for almost two minutes before he finally raised his head.

"Hello, Dr. Kirby," the Gunsmith greeted. "Looks like you're having fun tonight."

Kirby jerked his head around fearfully. Watery, red-rimmed eyes stared up at Clint from baggy lids. The doctor's shirt was stained with vomit. His lips trembled as he tried to speak.

"Wha . . . what are you doing here?" Kirby demanded, his eyes shifting to the gun in Clint's fist.

"I have to talk to you, Doc," the Gunsmith replied.

"With a gun?" Kirby asked with a shaky voice.

"I might need this gun," Clint told him, holstering the pistol. "I'm pretty sure somebody is going to try to kill you."

"Me?" Kirby recoiled against a wall. "But I haven't harmed anyone. I'm a medical man, a healer."

"And one of the founding fathers of Ten Pines," the Gunsmith added. "Just like Father Flynn and Sheriff Connors."

"But my son was the first victim," Kirby stated,

staggering across the room to grab a bottle from a shelf. "He was only a child when this town was built."

"He was your son, Doc," Clint snapped, quickly grabbing the bottle and taking it from Kirby's trembling grasp. "*Your* son. Edward and Sherman Colby were the mayor's sons. Of course, Father Flynn didn't have children and neither did Sheriff Connors. They couldn't be hurt by killing their sons, so they were murdered. I figure the killer won't be satisfied until he takes care of the last two names on the list. One of those names is yours."

"And the other one is mine?" a voice inquired.

Clint turned. Mayor Colby stood in the doorway, a Remington revolver in his fist. The Gunsmith placed his hand on his own pistol. Colby shook his head and slid his Remington into its holster.

"Relax, Adams," the mayor urged. "We're not enemies. I had my doubts about you until tonight. I saw you running toward the restaurant when the explosion occurred. I also saw Matt Connors pivot and drop, although I didn't realize he'd been shot at the time."

"I don't suppose you saw who shot him?" the Gunsmith remarked.

"No," Colby began, "but I'm not so sure I agree with your theory either. I understand this federal marshal came here looking for a crazed killer. In fact, he described the hunchback you saw at the livery."

"I don't trust Marshal Dobbs," Clint told Colby. "I asked Dobbs if I'd ever met him before. He told me we crossed paths in Windego. Then I told him I left before the Red Horse Saloon burned down. Asked him if he'd seen the fire."

"So?" Doc Kirby asked, confused by Clint's statement.

"So the Red Horse Saloon had burned down three

days *before* I arrived in Windego,'' Clint answered. ''They were still trying to clean up the mess when I was there. Dobbs lied about where he met me. He's also an unusual lawman. How many federal marshals do you figure would be able to saw off a man's arm as professionally as he did?''

''Perhaps he's better educated than most lawmen,'' Mayor Colby mused. ''After all, you seem to be well-read for a drifter.''

''Maybe,'' Clint allowed. ''But he still lied to me, and I don't trust him.''

''But what about the hunchback?'' Colby asked.

''Maybe there isn't a hunchback,'' the Gunsmith shrugged.

''But *you* saw him,'' the mayor insisted.

''I saw what looked like a hunchback,'' Clint said. ''But when you see a man with a beard and a big hump between his shoulder blades, that's about all you remember about his appearance. Could be somebody was counting on that. Now, I have a question for you, Doc.''

''Me?'' Kirby asked fearfully.

''What did you mean by that remark back in the church yesterday?'' Clint asked. ''What is 'the sin of this town'?''

''I . . . I was drunk,'' Kirby answered. ''I didn't know what I was saying.''

''Then I'll remind you what you said,'' Clint declared. ''You said your son was killed because of the great sin of this town. Colby, both your sons are dead, too. Now what the hell are you people trying to hide?''

''That's been our secret,'' Colby declared. ''Or, as Doc called it, our sin. But, I don't see how things can be any worse, so you might as well know everything. It happened over ten years ago, while we were still building Ten Pines."

"We didn't know we'd done anything wrong," Kirby interrupted as he reached for the bottle again.

"You can drink later, Doc," Clint replied, keeping the bottle away from him. "Right now it's time for all of us to be sober. Go on with the story, Mayor."

"Well, Ten Pines wasn't much to look at in those days," Colby continued. "Just a couple buildings. We put up the church first, then the jail. We were still building my house and the general store for Harlan Marshall when a drifter came into town. He was just a saddle bum, too lazy to work for a living. He sang and juggled and tried to entertain us, figuring we'd pay him for his talents. When he found out we wouldn't, he had to lower himself to accepting a job. Matt Connors was a carpenter as well as the sheriff back then. He took this kid on as an apprentice. I didn't care for him much, but some of the younger people liked him. Especially my daughter, Ellen."

"Do you remember this kid's name?" Clint asked.

"Tommy Gerard," Doc Kirby said. "I guess we never learned much else about him. Where he came from, why he was drifting. Never talked about his folks. We figured his family must'a been wiped out during the War."

"My daughter started to feel poorly," Colby began. "She threw up in the morning, and she gained a lot of weight. Eventually, it was obvious she was pregnant. Against her will, I took her to Doc. He confirmed it. I was furious. Reckon I was pretty hard on her when I found out, but hell, Adams, she was my only daughter, and she was only fourteen."

"Tommy was the father?" Clint asked.

"The Gerard kid was nineteen, a good-lookin' boy who always smiled and laughed," Colby said. "Ellen always seemed attracted to him. I was sure he'd made my daughter pregnant. We were all sure."

"*All* of you?" the Gunsmith raised his eyebrows.

"We took a vote," Colby said bitterly. "We voted whether or not Tommy was guilty. Doc, Matt Connors, Harlan Marshall, Father Flynn, and I—all of us agreed the kid did it. Looking back, only Father Flynn had any doubts. He wanted to hear the boy's story. Of course, Tommy denied it, but none of us believed him."

"Did you ask your daughter?" Clint asked.

"She was only fourteen, Adams," the mayor declared. "I couldn't see putting her through that. We were so sure we were right."

"We were so sure that we didn't hesitate to get a rope and hang that boy," Kirby interrupted.

"What would you do with a young bastard who raped your daughter, Adams?" Colby demanded. "So we killed him."

"But Tommy Gerard wasn't guilty," Kirby commented.

"I know he wasn't guilty, damn it!" the mayor snapped. "The morning after we hanged Tommy Gerard, Ellen disappeared. She ran off with Harlan Marshall's sixteen-year-old son. Ellen left a note which explained that Mike Marshall was the father of her baby. They run off because they were afraid we wouldn't let 'em stay together until they were old enough to get married. They were also afraid and disgusted by the way we lynched Tommy. I never saw her again or even received a letter from Ellen."

"They weren't the only ones who were repulsed by

what we done," Kirby said sadly. "Our wives could never forget that their husbands had murdered an innocent boy. Matt's wife and my wife ran out on us. Harlan's wife died before he did. Just seemed to waste away. Most of our children left, too. All of 'em except Joe, Edward, and Sherman. Now they're dead because of that awful crime we committed over a decade ago."

"That's nonsense, Doc," the mayor insisted. "Tommy Gerard was a goddamn drifter. Why would anyone want to avenge his death after all these years?"

"Maybe the killer will answer that question," Clint mused. "But we have to find him first."

"How do we do that?" Colby inquired.

A pistol suddenly exploded. Mayor Colby's head jerked violently as a large caliber projectile crashed into the back of his skull. His nose burst as the bullet kicked its way out the middle of his face.

TWENTY-SEVEN

The mayor's body wilted to the floor. Clint Adams' Colt revolver appeared in his hand faster than thought. He had drawn it instinctively, well-honed survival reflexes taking control of his actions.

A bearded figure stood in the shadows beyond the doorway, a Tranter pistol still in his fist. Clint swung his Colt toward the assassin and hastily fired a round at the killer. The gunman had already begun to retreat. The Gunsmith's slug splintered the wooden frame of the doorway, just shy of his mark.

The Gunsmith was about to take off after the killer, when a wooden keg suddenly rolled across the threshold, dumping several gallons of liquid across the floor. Clint recognized the substance by its familiar sharp odor.

Kerosene.

A match was tossed into the liquid, and it burst into flames. The blaze quickly spread as old newspapers and books caught fire. The killer didn't believe in taking chances. His ruthlessness was terrifying.

"Oh, my God!" Doc Kirby cried out. "We're gonna burn to death!"

The Gunsmith ignored him. The flames traveled along the floor and licked up the wallpaper. Smoke filled the enclosed area. The air was being burned up fast. Clint knew he'd have to act immediately, or he and the doctor would be a pair of charred corpses.

Clint found a stool near the table. Flames were already dancing along its wooden legs. The Gunsmith seized the furniture and promptly hurled it at the only window in the room. Flimsy framework and glass exploded. The icy night air rushed through the broken pane, fanning the flames.

"Move, damn it!" the Gunsmith growled as he grabbed Kirby's arm and steered the doctor toward the window.

He virtually pitched Kirby through the gap. The doctor hurtled outside and landed awkwardly in a snow drift. The Gunsmith felt intense heat scorch his left calf. He glanced down and saw flames licking his pants leg.

The Gunsmith dove through the window, and tumbled into the snow drift. The clammy cold embrace was a relief after narrowly escaping the inferno. Damp, cool snow quickly smothered the flames at his ankle.

Clint hauled Doc Kirby to his feet and towed him away from the burning building. A handful of townsfolk had cautiously approached the blazing structure. Harry was among the group, his Greener shotgun tucked under an arm just in case.

"Jesus Lord!" the bartender gasped. "This is one hell of a night!"

"Oh yeah?" the Gunsmith asked breathlessly. "Well, it isn't over yet—except for Mayor Colby. He's still in there."

"Burned alive?" Harry's eyes expanded with horror.

"Burned dead," Clint explained. "He'd already been shot through the head."

"Christ," the bartender muttered, "did you get the killer?"

"Not yet," the Gunsmith glancing at the faces of the rest of the group. He noticed Sandra among the crowd just before she spoke.

"Are you hurt, Clint?" the woman asked.

"I'm all right," he assured her. "Everybody better get back inside before we all freeze to death out here. Harry, can you look after the doctor?"

"I reckon so," the bartender replied. "You look like you could use a drink, Clint."

"If that's an offer," Clint said, "I accept."

The Gunsmith and Harry each grabbed one of Doc Kirby's arms and hauled him to the saloon. The rest of the townsfolk scurried for the shelter of their homes, hoping the ordeal would soon be over, and they'd survive the nightmare. No one even bothered to try to fight the fire at Kirby's home. The place wasn't close enough to any other buildings for the fire to spread, so they simply allowed it to burn itself out.

"Harry," Clint whispered, "I want you to take Doc inside your saloon. Then lock the place up as securely as possible. Don't let anybody in and keep that shotgun ready."

"All right, Clint," the bartender agreed. "What are you going to do?"

"I'm going to pay somebody a visit and see if I can find an answer or two," the Gunsmith told him. "With a little luck, we might have our killer before sunup."

"Yeah," Harry said grimly. "And if you ain't lucky, you'll get yourself killed."

"Well, if that happens," the Gunsmith replied, "I guess I won't be seeing you again."

Clint left Kirby with Harry and moved along the

plankwalk. He slipped around the corner of the saloon and crept into an alley. The Gunsmith slowly approached the building across the street, his hand poised on the butt of his Colt revolver. Clint noticed a light in one of the windows, but a thick curtain prevented him from peeking inside.

"Figures," Clint muttered to himself. "That'd be too easy."

The Gunsmith moved to the front of the general store. He rapped his knuckles on the door. Melissa Marshall opened it a mere crack. A single, pale green eye peered up at Clint and widened with surprise. Melissa opened the door wider.

"I know I told you to come back anytime," she said, "but I really didn't mean this late at night."

"Sorry about the hour," the Gunsmith replied. "But this is important."

"My aunt needs her rest," Melissa stated. "She's very upset by all the shooting and explosions and fires that have been going on tonight."

"Me, too," the Gunsmith replied. "I almost got my brains beat out, three different men tried to shoot me, almost got hit by flying shrapnel when the restaurant blew up, had to help cut a fella's arm off and about ten minutes ago I was nearly burned to death in a fire at Doc Kirby's house."

"I've been hearing all sorts of terrible noises," Melissa shook her head sadly. "I've been afraid to set foot outside since this started. Has the world gone mad?"

"Not the whole world," Clint answered, "just some of the people in it. Can you let me in?"

"I really don't know you very well, Clint," the woman answered. "I'm sorry, but I don't think I should let you in."

"Do you really think I'm a murderer?" Clint asked. "You'd do better to talk to me now than to take your chances with a lynch mob later."

"What do you mean?" Melissa frowned.

"Didn't your uncle ever tell you about this town?" Clint inquired. "They're fond of using ropes here."

"Come in," she decided at last. "But don't disturb Aunt Edith."

The Gunsmith entered the shop. Melissa closed the door and locked it, throwing a bolt in place. The woman wore a thick cotton robe, held together by a rope belt. She moved to the counter and struck a match to light a small kerosene lamp.

"Now what's this talk about lynching?" she asked, carrying the lantern from the counter.

"One happened here about ten years ago," the Gunsmith explained. "The good people of Ten Pines strung up a nineteen-year-old lad whom they accused of rape. Did you know about that?"

"I wouldn't think that would be too unusual out here in the West," Melissa commented, taking the lamp into the parlor. "Waiting for a circuit judge can take months, so I'm not surprised people take the law into their own hands from time to time."

"It isn't as common as you seem to think," Clint told her. "The youth they hanged was innocent. His name was Tommy Gerard."

"And you're going to protect me from the lynch mob, Clint?" Melissa inquired as she sat on the sofa, placing the lamp on an end table.

"Maybe you shouldn't be protected," the Gunsmith remarked, strolling into the room.

"You've certainly chosen an odd way to approach me, Clint," Melissa said with a sly grin. "It really isn't necessary, you know."

"What do you mean?" Clint asked, knitting his brow, moving next to the sofa.

"You want me, Clint," Melissa stated simply. "Just as I want you. We both sensed it the first time we met. Why be coy about it?"

Melissa slowly crossed her legs and purposely pulled open her robe to reveal the long naked limbs up to her hips. Clint gazed down at Melissa's beautifully shaped legs and creamy thighs. Her eyes fell upon his crotch, noticing the bulge between his legs.

"You might deny my words," she commented. "But you can't deny that."

Melissa extended a hand and patted Clint's groin. She casually unbuttoned his trousers to free his swollen member. The woman was right. Clint wanted her. Melissa was a very attractive and sexy lady. His cock throbbed as she stroked it.

Then Clint heard the faint sound of an object creaking against the floorboards. He abruptly disengaged himself from Melissa, shoving her away from him roughly. Clint quickly turned around, his limp penis dangling from his open trousers as his hand went to the .45 Colt on his hip.

The gray-haired figure seated in the wheelchair stared at Clint through the smoked lenses of the glasses perched on a hawk-billed nose. Aunt Edith's mouth fell open. The Gunsmith hastily tucked his member inside his pants and buttoned his fly.

"Good evening, ma'am," he said sheepishly. "Uh . . . I hope we didn't wake you."

TWENTY-EIGHT

"What sort of disgraceful immoral behavior are you two indulged in?" Edith demanded, drawing her shawl around her neck and throat. "This is my home and you dare to engage in . . . under my roof! I'm going to have the sheriff arrest you, young man."

"The sheriff is dead," Clint Adams replied dryly.

"Clint," Melissa gasped, "my aunt has a weak heart. Don't upset her."

"Your 'aunt' knows goddamn good and well the sheriff is dead," the Gunsmith said gruffly.

"Watch your language, you fornicator!" Edith insisted, her reedy voice almost cracking. "Melissa, get this man out of here. I don't want you whoring about anymore, young lady."

"Oh, Auntie!" Melissa sobbed. "How can you say something like that!"

The young woman bolted into the general store section, her face buried in her hands. The Gunsmith shook his head as he turned to face Edith.

"She's overacting," Clint declared. "You should have taught her better."

Suddenly, Clint drew his Colt and aimed it at Edith's face. His thumb cocked back the hammer. This wasn't necessary with a double-action revolver, but it served to emphasize his threat.

173

"My God," Edith rasped. "He's gone mad! Melissa, get help! This maniac has just pulled a gun on me!"

"Keep your hands high," the Gunsmith warned. "You reach for that blanket, and I'll blow your head off."

"Clint!" Melissa exclaimed as she rushed back into the room. "You *really are* threatening to kill my aunt! Put that gun away this instant!"

"I think your aunt wears a scarf to hide an Adam's apple," Clint announced. "And I think 'she' has a wig on 'her' head to appear to be an old woman."

The Gunsmith glanced at Melissa. She stood with both arms folded over her chest. Clint shifted the aim of his Colt to cover the young woman, although he watched Edith with the corner of his eye.

"And," he continued. "I think you got a gun while you were in the general store. If you don't drop it and raise you're hands, I'll have to put a bullet between those lovely breasts of yours."

Melissa slowly unfolded her arms and dropped a .22 Sharps pepperbox pistol. She raised her hands. The woman glared at the Gunsmith, her eyes ablaze with hatred.

"Well, 'Aunt Edith'," Clint sighed, "either prove you're a woman or admit you're a man—a man named Thurgood Gerard."

"Very good, Mr. Adams," the figure in the wheelchair commented, the voice suddenly quite masculine.

The person who had been known as Aunt Edith calmly tossed aside the scarf and removed a gray wig to reveal close-cropped brown hair. He took off the smoked glasses and gazed up at Clint through pale green eyes.

"How did you figure out who I really am?" Gerard inquired, rising from the wheelchair.

"Your disguises were pretty good," Clint admitted. "The bearded hunchback pretending to be drunk was clever. Then you showed up again disguised as Marshal Sam Dobbs, hunting 'John Bates', a name for your own hunchback character. Who'd ever suspect a man hunting for himself?"

"I think you suspected me when you said I looked familiar," Gerard shrugged. "I suppose that question about Windego and the Red Horse Saloon was a trap?"

"Yeah," the Gunsmith nodded.

"Oh, dear," Gerard sighed as he shook his head. "How did you recognize me? I thought my makeup was adequate."

"Everything was perfect," Clint assured him, "except that Edith, the Bates hunchback, and Marshal Dobbs all had the same nose."

"A rather large nose," Gerard commented. "Difficult to make a large nose look smaller. Making a smaller nose larger is considerably easier."

"But that hawk-like profile gives you a striking image as Hamlet on those posters," Clint stated. "That's when I first saw your face. A bartender named Pete in Carsontown was looking forward to your Shakespeare performances. When I see him, I'll tell Pete that you're certainly a very good actor."

"I thought I overheard you mention to Melissa— that is her real name, by the way, but the last name is Gerard—that you were aware Tommy Gerard had been lynched for a crime he didn't commit."

"That's right," the Gunsmith nodded. "Mayor Colby and Doc Kirby told me the whole story before you charged in with that flaming kerosene trick. When they mentioned Tommy Gerard, I remembered the poster for Thurgood Gerard the actor. Who else would be able to disguise himself well enough to play three different roles in this town and *almost* get away with murder?''

"Murder?'' Gerard raised an eyebrow. "The men who hanged my son committed murder. I sought justice. Call it revenge if you wish. Revenge and justice are often one and the same.''

"Joe Kirby and the Colby boys were children when Tommy was lynched,'' the Gunsmith stated. "They didn't have anything to do with their fathers' actions.''

"By killing the sons first,'' Gerard began, "their fathers suffered just as I suffered when Thomas was murdered.''

"Which doesn't make you any better than they were,'' Clint told him. "In fact, you're worse, because at least the people of Ten Pines *thought* Tommy was guilty. You *knew* Joe, Edward, and Sherman were innocent.''

"I made the punishment fit the crime,'' Gerard declared.

"And now you're trying to justify cold-blooded murder,'' Clint said. "How can you justify killing Lilly?''

"That was an accident,'' Gerard insisted.

"I bet the people of Ten Pines would have said the same about why they hanged Tommy,'' the Gunsmith replied.

"Doesn't it matter to you that I saved your life in the saloon?'' Gerard inquired.

"Yeah,'' Clint nodded, "and you tried to kill me at Doc Kirby's place. That sort of cancels everything out, doesn't it?''

"Actually," Gerard mused, "my revenge was pretty successful. Harlan Marshall died before I could catch up with him, but I killed all the others except Dr. Kirby. Kirby is an alcoholic and he's lost his only son and his home and place of business. He'll surely drink himself to death within a year now. So, if you let us go, it'll all be over, Adams."

"Let you go?" the Gunsmith scoffed. "Why should I do that?"

"Maybe I can make it worthwhile," Melissa suggested as she approached Clint. "My father will understand. He sees nothing wrong with my having a healthy sex life with a certain amount of variety in partners."

She suddenly untied her belt and slipped the robe from her shoulders. The garment fell to the floor. Melissa stood before Clint in all her naked beauty, the perk nipples of her breasts aimed at the Gunsmith.

Thurgood Gerard immediately took advantage of his daughter's distraction tactic. His right hand swung to the small of his back where a .32 Colt pistol was thrust into the hoop of his skirt. The actor drew the pistol as Clint noticed the motion.

The Gunsmith squeezed the trigger of his .45, but Melissa had lunged forward and caught his wrist, jerking Clint's arm toward the floor. The modified Colt fired a harmless round into the carpet.

Clint Adams glanced up and saw the muzzle of Gerard's revolver pointing at his face.

TWENTY-NINE

The Gunsmith had tangled with a lot of unusual opponents, but this was the first time he'd been attacked by a man in a dress and a naked woman at the same time. It might be the last time it ever happened to him unless he could prevent getting a .32 slug through his forehead.

Clint reacted swiftly, following the natural impulse to swing his own Colt revolver back on target to blast Thurgood Gerard before the actor could fire a shot. Melissa still clung to Clint's wrist, and he pulled her forward between himself and Gerard.

The sharp crack of a small caliber pistol erupted. Melissa stiffened, her eyes expressing more astonishment than pain as a bullet struck her in the back. The bullet drilled a tunnel under her left shoulder blade and punctured her heart.

"No!" Thurgood Gerard shrieked with grief and rage.

The killer suddenly charged into his daughter's rapidly dying body. He used Melissa as a battering ram and drove her into Clint Adams. The unexpected tactic caught the Gunsmith off guard, and the modified Colt revolver fell from Clint's hand to the floor somewhere behind him.

Melissa's corpse crumbled to the carpet. Thurgood

Gerard raised his pistol, but Clint grabbed the actor's wrist before he could take aim. Gerard's left fist slammed hard into the Gunsmith's jaw.

Clint held onto his opponent's wrist and twisted it with both hands. Gerard's fingers lost their grip on the Colt, and it fell to the floor. The actor's fist hammered a blow to Clint's neck. The Gunsmith felt the room whirl into a dizzy blur.

Gerard suddenly ripped the long black skirt from his waist and flung it over the Gunsmith's head. The veil of cotton covered Clint's eyes, blinding him to two vicious punches. Clint tasted blood as the blows knocked him backward.

The Gunsmith thrust an arm high and successfully threw off the skirt. The first thing he saw was Gerard's fist heading toward his face. Hard knuckles crashed into his jaw and sent the Gunsmith staggering backward into a wall.

Gerard snarled like a rabid beast as he thrust clawed fingers at Clint's face, trying to jam both thumbs into the Gunsmith's eyes. Clint's lightning reflexes saved him from having his eyeballs gouged from their sockets. He snared Gerard's wrists, closing a fist around each to hold back the talon-like assault.

The Gunsmith kicked in Gerard's crotch. The actor groaned and doubled up in agony. Clint hooked his left fist to Gerard's face and followed with a solid right cross. The killer's head bounced from the punches, his knees buckling under him.

Clint cocked back his fist, eager to finish off his demented adversary with another right cross. Suddenly, Gerard reached forward and seized Clint's sheepskin jacket in both fists. He pulled forcibly, dropped down on one buttock, and raised a foot to the

Gunsmith's midsection. The actor straightened his knee and sent Clint hurtling head-over-heels onto the carpet.

The Gunsmith rolled with the fall and rose unsteadily to his feet. His vision was hazy and distorted. Thurgood Gerard resembled a two-headed demon with four arms as he approached Clint Adams. The bruises he received during the previous fight with Thrasher and Crusher throbbed painfully as the Gunsmith backed away from the bizzare creature which threatened to tear him limb from limb.

Clint's vision cleared abruptly. When Gerard lashed a fist at the Gunsmith's face, Clint was ready for him. The Gunsmith dodged the punch and grabbed the actor's arm. He yanked Gerard forward and jammed a shoulder into his opponent's armpit. Clint bent his back and straightened his knees. The killer sailed over the Gunsmith's shoulder and flew six feet before he smashed into the floor.

Thurgood Gerard scrambled to all fours and tried to rise. Clint Adams stepped forward and kicked the actor in the face. Gerard tumbled across the floor, but he sprang upright, fierce anger still in his eyes in spite of the fact his front teeth had been shattered by Clint's boot.

The killer lunged at Clint, and dove face-first into the Gunsmith's fist. The punch propelled him backward into his own wheelchair. Man and chair rolled rapidly across the bedroom floor until it crashed into a wall.

The Gunsmith wearily shuffled across the threshold into the bedroom. He thrust both hands into the pockets of his sheepskin jacket. Thurgood Gerard slowly dragged himself from the wheelchair and fell to his knees by the foot of a bed. Blood dripped from the actor's gaping mouth. His broken jaw hung awkwardly as he leaned against the bed, panting hard.

"It's over, Gerard," Clint told him. "You're through."

Gerard nodded weakly. He clawed at the bedpost and gradually pulled himself to his feet. Gerard leaned forward, sliding a hand under the mattress. The actor suddenly pulled a Tranter revolver from its hiding place.

The killer thrust his pistol at the Gunsmith and thumbed back the hammer. Clint Adams' hand emerged from the pocket of his jacket. He held the Remington derringer he'd taken from Richard O'Shea earlier that night.

The report of the gunshot echoed within the room. A .41-caliber bullet struck Thurgood Gerard between the eyes. The slug split his skull and destroyed his brain. The actor was dead before he could squeeze the trigger of his Tranter.

THIRTY

"I can hardly believe the last couple days really happened," Harry commented as he poured a shot of whiskey for the Gunsmith and another one for himself. "Imagine so many folks gettin' killed because of somethin' that happened so long ago."

"It wasn't such a long time ago to Thurgood Gerard," the Gunsmith replied as he leaned against the bar and raised the glass to his lips. "He must have had an obsession with finding his son after Tommy wandered out West over ten years ago. When he found out what had happened to his son, that obsession became one of revenge."

"How do you figure he found out about the lynching?" the bartender asked.

"Well, I doubt that we'll ever know for sure," Clint replied. "But I guess he probably met up with Ellen Colby and Mike Marshall."

"The two kids who ran off after the lynchin'?"

"Yeah," the Gunsmith answered. "He seemed to know a lot about this town, and he knew enough about the Marshall family to impersonate Harlan's sister Edith. Hard to say how long he was in Utah gathering information so he could come here and settle his old score with the founders of Ten Pines."

"But didn't you say you saw posters for Gerard and

his acting company supposedly coming here on tour to perform some sort of play?'' Harry asked.

"That's right," Clint confirmed. "But the tour was canceled because Gerard had disappeared. Now, if he had succeeded in getting away with the murders and somebody found out Tommy had been hanged in Ten Pines, Thurgood Gerard would have looked awful suspicious if his acting company had been in Utah at the time. If anybody had asked where he was during that time, I'm sure he could have had enough witnesses bought and paid for to swear he was with them in order to please any investigation which might have followed."

"And he dragged his daughter around with him to help get revenge on the folks who lynched his son," Harry frowned. "I bet that poor gal didn't have much of a life."

"Melissa was only about twenty so she was probably less than ten years old when Tommy was killed," Clint mused. "If Gerard's obsession began when Tommy left home, that means Melissa spent more than half her life having her father's notions shoved down her throat. Instead of taking care of the child he had left, Gerard ruined her life as well as his own."

"What's really strange to me is the way Gerard behaved when he was playin' at bein' Sam Dobbs," Harry stated. "I'm not sure I would have believed your story if you hadn't shown me those disguises in Gerard's chest at the general store. 'Cause, well, I liked Sam Dobbs. I admired the way he took over amputating O'Shea's arm."

"Gerard murdered a lot of people," Clint began, "but he honestly believed it was justified. He wasn't really bad as much as he was crazy. He even saved

Richard O'Shea's life, and he saved mine, too. That's something we can't forget when we remember Thurgood Gerard."

"Reckon you're right," Harry agreed. "How long you gonna be in Ten Pines, Clint? You're welcome to stay as long as you like, but you ain't gonna find much gunsmithin' work here."

"If it doesn't start snowing again, I'll probably leave tomorrow. If the weather gets too rough, I'll wait it out. What the hell. Right now staying at the hotel and using the livery for free, while everybody insists on giving me meals and liquor at half price, makes Ten Pines not a bad place to wait at."

"Speakin' of liquor," Harry grinned. "You want another drink, Clint?"

"No, thanks," the Gunsmith said. "But if you have a bottle and a couple glasses for sale, I'd be obliged."

"*Two* glasses?" Harry raised his eyebrows.

"Just figured I'd see if Sandra feels like some company tonight," the Gunsmith said with a shrug.

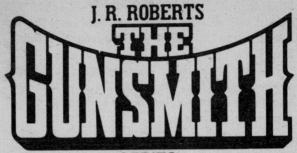

J. R. ROBERTS
THE GUNSMITH

SERIES

☐ 30929-1	THE GUNSMITH #20: THE DODGE CITY GANG	$2.50
☐ 30910-0	THE GUNSMITH #21: SASQUATCH HUNT	$2.50
☐ 30894-5	THE GUNSMITH #23: THE RIVERBOAT GANG	$2.25
☐ 30895-3	THE GUNSMITH #24: KILLER GRIZZLY	$2.50
☐ 30896-1	THE GUNSMITH #25: NORTH OF THE BORDER	$2.50
☐ 30897-X	THE GUNSMITH #26: EAGLE'S GAP	$2.50
☐ 30899-6	THE GUNSMITH #27: CHINATOWN HELL	$2.50
☐ 30900-3	THE GUNSMITH #28: THE PANHANDLE SEARCH	$2.50
☐ 30902-X	THE GUNSMITH #29: WILDCAT ROUND-UP	$2.50
☐ 30903-8	THE GUNSMITH #30: THE PONDEROSA WAR	$2.50
☐ 30904-6	THE GUNSMITH #31: TROUBLE RIDES A FAST HORSE	$2.50
☐ 30911-9	THE GUNSMITH #32: DYNAMITE JUSTICE	$2.50
☐ 30912-7	THE GUNSMITH #33: THE POSSE	$2.50
☐ 30913-5	THE GUNSMITH #34: NIGHT OF THE GILA	$2.50
☐ 30914-3	THE GUNSMITH #35: THE BOUNTY WOMEN	$2.50
☐ 30915-1	THE GUNSMITH #36: BLACK PEARL SALOON	$2.50
☐ 30935-6	THE GUNSMITH #37: GUNDOWN IN PARADISE	$2.50
☐ 30936-4	THE GUNSMITH #38: KING OF THE BORDER	$2.50
☐ 30940-2	THE GUNSMITH #39: THE EL PASO SALT WAR	$2.50

Prices may be slightly higher in Canada.

Available at your local bookstore or return this form to:

 CHARTER BOOKS
Book Mailing Service
P.O. Box 690, Rockville Centre, NY 11571

Please send me the titles checked above. I enclose _____. Include 75¢ for postage and handling if one book is ordered; 25¢ per book for two or more not to exceed $1.75. California, Illinois, New York and Tennessee residents please add sales tax.

NAME_____

ADDRESS_____

CITY_____STATE/ZIP_____

(allow six weeks for delivery.)   A1/a